HEARTS IN PERIL™

Christmas Conspiracy

Pamela Tracy

Annie's®

AnniesFiction.com

Books in the Hearts in Peril series

Christmas Conspiracy
Copyright © 2023 Annie's.

The characters and events in this book are fictional, and any resemblance to actual persons or events is coincidental.

Library of Congress-in-Publication Data
Christmas Conspiracy / by Pamela Tracy
p. cm.
I. Title
2022942364

AnniesFiction.com
(800) 282-6643
Hearts in Peril™
Series Creator: Shari Lohner
Series Editor: Amy Woods

10 11 12 13 14 | Printed in China | 9 8 7 6 5 4 3 2 1

$\mathcal{R}$achel Andrews's foot slipped off the gas pedal for a moment. She whispered, "Nostalgia," and earned a snort from Timber as she expertly regained control of her vehicle.

"It is nostalgia," she informed Timber, who seemed a little judgmental about the car's brief slide in the snow. The dog was too smart for his own good.

The minute Rachel hit the outskirts of her hometown, strong emotions had settled inside her. Maybe if she repeated the word enough, she'd convince herself it was just nostalgia that was causing the lump in her throat.

Maybe it was the snow in Grandma's yard—pristine, perfect, and bereft, reminding Rachel of past snowball fights and laughter.

Rachel didn't want to cry, but she couldn't help it. Nostalgia was an equal-opportunity emotion, bringing both the highs and lows of powerful memories.

"These are tears of joy," she told herself. "I'm home."

Timber—her black, beige, and brown German shepherd-husky mix, trained as a search and rescue dog—watched her from the passenger seat. His expression implied he knew that her tears had nothing to do with joy.

Tears of fear was more likely. Fear of messing up and losing more than she'd already lost, which was why Rachel had purposely arrived at a predawn hour on Sunday, a day early, planning to park her gray SUV behind Grandma's house so her family wouldn't know she was there.

She needed some time to reflect, time to deal with her insecurities and frustrations over the past, before heading to her parents' lodge and delving into her big sister's wedding chaos.

Grandma Nettie would have understood. She would have comforted Rachel with phrases like "Let bygones be bygones," and "Forgiveness is a stream that runs both ways."

The tires on Rachel's SUV slid a bit on the dirt road, then dug into the snow, cresting a driveway that luckily had already been shoveled. That would have been Rachel's dad's doing. He'd wanted her to stay at the lodge instead of his mother's house, but when she begged off, he'd made sure to prepare the cabin.

A whole year later, and still the family couldn't bring themselves to go through Nettie's house and pack up the memories left to them. Rachel was every bit as guilty, especially since the house had been left to her. She'd been present for the reading of the will. Rachel had inherited Nettie's home while her sister, Emily, had inherited Nettie's money. Both would rather have Nettie. Afterward, Rachel had fled back to Cave Creek, Arizona.

Her dad had been so helpful, keeping the utilities on and the exterior maintained until she decided what to do.

She parked, switched off the ignition, and stepped from the SUV, gazing at the century-old home. Timber followed, tired of being cooped up in the car.

Much to Rachel's regret, she hadn't been there to say goodbye to Nettie. She could have held her grandma's hand, offered comfort, acknowledged that staying away so long had been a mistake.

And staying away hadn't allowed Rachel to bridge the chasm that separated her and her sister. She hoped that the week leading up to Emily's wedding would right past wrongs and unite the family.

In addition to mending fences with Emily, Rachel's number one goal was to make her sister feel special during her wedding week.

Timber growled and pushed past her, blocking her from moving. "Timber, what—"

Boom!

The explosion came from nowhere. Rachel instinctively covered her ears and dropped to her knees. The air turned from frigid to acrid, and pieces of wood, rock, and glass pelted her and mingled with the falling snow. She scrambled, crawling, until she was completely shielded by the SUV's open front passenger door. The palms of her hands grew numb as they pressed against hard packed snow. A brief wave of heat hit and then retreated. Timber crowded next to her. Amid the dirt and stone, something shiny landed on her hand. A necklace?

She pushed herself to a crouch, swept hair off her face, and peered over the top of the door. A corner of her grandmother's house was gone. Smoke billowed from the door-sized hole.

She rescued the necklace from the snow, shoved it in the back pocket of her jeans, and climbed back into the SUV, letting out a breath as the shock subsided and adrenaline kicked in. She grabbed her cell phone from the charger. No service. Even the telecommunication giants couldn't beat the combined power of mountains, tall trees, and a snowstorm. Her grandma's house had a landline, but she wasn't going into an unstable environment to call the fire department.

"Timber, in," she commanded. She needed to get to the nearest house, which belonged to the Scott family. Their son, Cody, had been Emily's high school boyfriend and Rachel's friend. With any luck, the boom had awakened them, and they'd already called the fire department.

Instead of obeying as he normally would, Timber used body language to give Rachel an alert.

Alarmed, Rachel touched the top of the dog's head. She hadn't set a scent for Timber to track, but after handling her dog for so long, she trusted him enough to follow his direction.

A bulky figure scurried away from the house, headed toward the snow-laden foliage of the Arapahoe National Forest.

Rachel didn't stop to think. Instead, adrenaline and a budding anger that someone would intentionally damage her grandma's house compelled her to ignore years of search and rescue training to never pursue a threat alone. She flung herself out of the SUV and into snow so deep it slid over the tops of her boots. Timber dashed through the unblemished snow ahead of her, not at all bothered by the cold or uneven ground.

By the time Rachel made it to the backyard, all she could see was a retreating figure wearing a black coat. When he glanced over his shoulder, Rachel took note of his appearance. Male, white, tall, and left-handed—or at least that was how he carried his gun.

He had such a lead, she couldn't possibly catch him. If she were on a search and rescue mission, she'd have binoculars and a firearm. But her current job titles were daughter, bridesmaid, and sister instead. All she had in her SUV was her winter outerwear, wedding gifts, and clothing. Well, she did have pepper spray safely tucked in the glove box.

Shivering, she managed a few more steps, the cold slapping against her cheeks and burning her lips. Why hadn't she grabbed her coat before giving chase?

Ahead of her, Timber yelped and stood still, holding his front right paw in the air.

Rachel made it to her canine companion's side and dropped to her knees, checking the man's progress one last time before gently taking Timber's paw in her palm to examine it.

Then something heavy landed on the back of her head, the snow rose up to meet her, and darkness fell over her like a blanket.

"You have two problems," Bob Lewis told Cody Scott, coming to stand beside him.

Cody frowned. He'd been back in Rolling Pine, Colorado, all of two minutes, fresh off an all-night standoff with a fugitive back in Denver. He'd only pulled into the Gas 'n' Go because, well, he'd needed gas and a bottled water.

"Both of your problems are big," Bob went on, looking down at his dog, Biggles, as if expecting the mutt to agree with him.

At the moment, Cody was willing to agree with anything Bob said. His most fervent wish was to head to his parents' house and sleep for twenty-four hours straight. Then he'd head over to the Rocky Mountains Lodge and congratulate his ex-high school girlfriend on her upcoming marriage. The timing of the invitation to her wedding couldn't have been better. It put Cody in the exact area where the United States Marshals hoped to locate a high-profile financial criminal rumored to be in the area.

Rolling Pine occupied fifty square miles and boasted a year-round population of about ten thousand. At times, tourists more than doubled the population, whether they were white-water rafting or skiing. A lot of money came with the tourists.

"Big problems," Bob repeated, stretching out his bare hands before shoving them into the front pockets of his black coat. He began rocking back and forth in too-big, untied shoes.

Bob wasn't big on change. The longtime Rolling Pine resident still lived near the cabin his parents had built, sans indoor plumbing. When the county said Bob would have to succumb to the housing maintenance code, he'd moved a ramshackle RV onto his property, stuck a *Condemned* sign in the front window of the cabin, and proceeded to live in both.

"You going to tell me what my problems are, Bob?" Cody asked, stifling a grin as he topped off the gas tank in his green Jeep Wrangler and returned the nozzle. He peeled off his gloves and handed them to Bob, who took them eagerly but didn't put them on.

Cody knew better than to press. Bob was a fixture of Rolling Pine who had to be well over seventy. He'd never married, never worked more than an odd job or two, and was completely harmless, if a bit eccentric.

Bob continued, "Someone should have gotten in touch with you. I mean, you being a town hero and all."

Cody wasn't a town hero. He'd played football, enlisted in the army, returned stateside with scars invisible to the naked eye, joined the police force, and had then become a US Marshal. Most people in town didn't know about the scars or the US Marshal job. Some things were best kept quiet.

Bob, though, loved high school football and remembered Cody's glory days. He'd lived in Rolling Pine since it had boasted a population of 213 and knew a little about everything and everyone.

Cody opened the Wrangler's driver's side door and started to get in. He was so tired, his hands were starting to shake—and not because of the missing gloves and frigid air.

The early hour meant deserted streets and unopened businesses. Bob, however, was wide awake. "I would have called," he mused, "but I can't find my phone."

According to Cody's parents, the mayor of Rolling Pine had purchased Bob a cell phone and personally taught him how to use it. It made for a good story on the town's website. But so far, no one knew how to help Bob keep track of the phone.

"I didn't lose the power bank though," Bob bragged, patting a small white stuffed dog clipped to the backpack he always carried.

"That's a power bank?"

Bob nodded. "Miss Shelley at the library gave it to me. Said she knew I would never lose it because it looks like my dog."

A blond Labrador mix named Biggles had been Bob's sidekick since Cody was in high school, never missing a football game.

"First problem," Bob continued, "is Emily."

Cody froze. "Why is Emily a problem?"

"She's getting married to Justin and not to you," Bob said matter-of-factly.

"That's okay. I'm here for the wedding. I hear she's marrying a great guy."

"But you were supposed to marry her. He's nice, though. Takes me to breakfast sometimes.

"I dated her, Bob, but we're friends now," Cody said gently. "We went our separate ways a long time ago."

Bob grumbled something under his breath.

Cody left the door open but fired up the engine. The sound would either inspire Bob to share what the second problem was or encourage him to save it for another day. For the past twenty-four hours, Cody had been pulling stakeout duty, sitting in a car. His back hurt, his fingers cramped, and he hadn't had a good night's sleep in far too long. He was in no mood for Bob's ramblings.

Bob cocked his head. "The second problem is there's smoke on the mountain, around your parents' neighborhood."

Cody's eyes shot to the horizon, where he spotted a billow of smoke. *Fire!*

Cody hopped in the front seat of his Jeep, quickly radioed in the fire, and in moments was on the county road leading home.

When he made the first turn, he recognized the house on fire. Not his parents' but the one that had belonged to their late neighbor, Nettie Andrews. His mother had often bemoaned how it had stood empty since Nettie died. At least that meant there wouldn't be casualties.

Then he saw it—a gray SUV parked in the driveway with one door open. He slid his Jeep in behind it and jumped to the ground. His boots crunched in the snow as he jogged to the SUV. The front passenger seat had a blanket covered with dog hair spread over it. A red dog bowl was on the floorboard. The back seat held two suitcases, a Bible, a bag of snacks, a winter coat, a scarf, and mittens. He could see a dog crate in the hatchback.

As if on cue, he heard barking.

Cody took off running. Both paw and footprints trailed around the house instead of to the door. As he rounded the house, he saw a big German shepherd mix standing guard over a woman sprawled facedown in the snow. All Cody could tell was that she had black hair and wore a red shirt.

As Cody rushed to the woman's side, he noticed that the dog held its paw in the air. The poor guy was probably injured, but he gave Cody the impression that the woman had a protector who would take Cody down if need be.

First things first—take it slow and gain the dog's trust.

"It's okay, boy. You've got to let me check on your owner first, then I'll tend to you."

The dog growled in warning but backed up to allow Cody to reach his owner. Cody went to his knees to examine the woman. He checked her vitals as well as he could without moving her, the dog watching his every move. Her breathing was good and her pulse normal, but she was unconscious, her hair matted with blood, and there was a good-sized hematoma on the back of her head. When there was no more he could do, he gently rolled her onto her back.

His breath caught. It was Rachel Andrews.

"—and a mild concussion." Words, spoken in a deep voice that Rachel did not recognize, ebbed and flowed. She kept her eyes closed. Opening them didn't seem like a good idea.

" . . . not life-threatening . . ." continued the voice.

Maybe she should open her eyes. She tried, but nothing happened. It almost felt as if she were weighed down with something heavy and hot. Whatever was under her was hard and uncomfortable. The room smelled like cleaning supplies. She tried to move her fingers and they hurt. Moving her head wasn't an option.

The mysterious owner of the deep voice had more to say. "She'll probably have a headache. You'll want to watch her tonight. The loss of consciousness concerns me."

It concerned Rachel too.

"You might notice her having trouble concentrating," the speaker added.

Rachel decided to concentrate on keeping her eyes closed even though she was curious about who was talking.

"She'll be forgetful."

Rachel closed her eyes even tighter. She needed to remember something. Finally, it clicked, and she croaked, "Timber."

"Sweetheart, are you awake?" Her mother's voice.

"I'm awake."

That was all the encouragement Rachel's mom, Virginia, needed. "We were so worried. We didn't expect you until tomorrow.

Why didn't you tell us you were coming into town early? How do you feel?"

"I can tell you how Rachel feels," Rachel's dad, Dennis, joked. "Like she doesn't know which question to answer first. So I'll ask just one. How are you feeling, honey?"

"I'm okay. Where's Timber?"

"If you mean your dog," came another voice, one that sounded vaguely familiar, "I took him to Dr. Levy. He has a pretty deep cut on one front paw. Didn't stop him from guarding you though."

Rachel opened her eyes. Her whole family, somewhat blurry, stared back at her. Her sister, Emily, leaned against a tall stranger. That must be her fiancé, Justin Fletcher.

Then, there was Cody Scott, handsome as ever. Maybe even more handsome than she remembered. He was the one who had spoken, assuring her that her dog was safe at the vet.

Quickly, she switched her gaze to the doctor, who immediately stepped forward to shine a light in her eyes, making the headache worse.

Rachel closed her eyes, willed the nausea away, then reopened them. Nothing had changed, and Cody was still leaning against the wall as if a decade hadn't passed and he was part of the family.

Great, Rachel thought. The first time she'd seen him in years and she was at the Rolling Pine Emergency Clinic with wet, matted hair, and a headache the size of Texas.

"Is Timber all right?"

"He'll be fine," Cody said. "It was as if he understood that we were taking care of you. He even let my dad wrap him in the blanket you had in your back seat. They're already at the animal hospital."

Rachel's dad moved next to the bed and patted her arm. "Volunteer fire department got to your grandma's house in time to stop the fire before it spread. Cody called them as he was leaving the gas station."

"I can't believe you saw the fire from there." Emily—tall, regal, beautiful—tugged the man next to her toward Rachel. "I'm so glad you're home. Not quite like this, though."

Rachel tried to nod, but even the smallest movement made her dizzy.

Emily went on. "This is Justin. I was hoping to introduce you under better circumstances."

"I'm glad you're all right," Justin said.

Rachel closed her eyes, counted to ten, and opened them again. A wave of pain washed over her. She closed her eyes again. As if reading her mind, Dad patted her arm again.

"I didn't spot the fire. Bob Lewis did," Cody told everyone.

"What were you doing with Bob?" Rachel's mom raised an eyebrow.

"I was getting gas. He and Biggles happened to walk by."

"How bad is Grandma Nettie's house?" Rachel asked.

"Most of the damage seemed to be around the hallway and bathroom," Cody said.

"We're thinking the water heater blew," her dad said. "I noticed some corrosion and had already called Chris Mack to come look at it. He said he'd be out tomorrow. I had no idea you'd be here today, or I would have made sure it was ready before you arrived."

"The water heater?" Rachel tried to wrap her mind around his words.

"You're kidding," Justin said in disbelief. "A water heater can simply explode like that? Someone could have been killed."

"It happens more often than you'd think," Cody said.

Emily moved next to Rachel and gave her a hug. "I'm glad you're all right. I'm sorry about Grandma Nettie's house."

"The cabin can be repaired," Cody assured. "The damage was largely contained to one corner."

"And updating that bathroom will be a good thing," her dad added.

Clearing her throat, Rachel tried to sound more in control. "The water heater exploded. Is that what hit me? Or was it that man?"

"Man?" everyone echoed at once, including the doctor.

Cody closed his eyes for a moment, tried to reconstruct the environment as he'd seen it while running toward Rachel. He hadn't spotted a man, but—

"I'd just pulled up in the driveway and got out when something exploded," Rachel explained. "I took cover and went for my phone, but then I saw a man running from the cabin toward the woods."

"And you chased him?" Virginia scolded. "What were you thinking?"

"You could have been killed," Emily added.

Dennis calmly patted his younger daughter's arm. Cody remembered how alike Rachel and her father were, whereas Emily was more like her mother.

"This might be one time," Dennis said, "where you needed to stop and think before acting."

"I know. I was so surprised and upset that I reacted without thinking it through first," Rachel said.

While Rachel shared what little she remembered, Cody called the chief of police, Kevin Becker. Since the police station was next door, Cody figured Becker would arrive shortly.

When he hung up, he found the Andrews clan debating whether to head to the cabin to find out the extent of the damage. Fortunately, Dennis was opposed to the idea. "We'll go when the fire department tells us it's safe."

"Snow would have tempered any residual fires," Virginia argued. "When I think of Nettie's belongings wet and ruined—"

"We can go check the outside from a safe distance," Justin offered.

Next to him, Emily frowned at her watch. "We're meeting the disc jockey about the reception in an hour."

"We can call him and reschedule," Justin said. "Surely he'll understand."

Cody spoke up. "If Rachel witnessed a burglar or an arsonist fleeing Nettie's house, then it's a crime scene and the chief won't want you to disturb anything."

"Why would anybody break into Nettie's place?" Virginia asked. "She didn't have anything valuable, but I hope her furniture is all right. Emily, maybe you should reschedule and head over there."

A voice boomed from the doorway, surprising everyone. "It's not a good idea," announced police chief Kevin Becker. Moving over to Rachel's bed, he asked, "How are you doing?"

"I'll be fine. Slight concussion."

"She has quite a bump on the back of her head," the doctor added. "Plus abrasions on her hands and knees. Thanks to Cody, she got here quickly. Apart from a headache, dizziness, and some nausea, she should be good to go in a few hours."

"Good. I'm glad it wasn't worse." Chief Becker turned to address the room. "I have a deputy cordoning off the area around the cabin. I don't want any of you there without me or until the fire inspector signs off, which will be tomorrow at the earliest."

Rachel immediately said, "I should be the one to go."

Cody's throat went dry at the thought of Rachel returning to where she'd been injured, and an unexpected urge to protect her tugged at his chest.

"Absolutely not," Virginia responded. "Tomorrow you'll still be resting."

"I can go," Emily offered.

"I'll be fine," Rachel protested, trying to push herself up on her elbows. "A few hours will have passed."

Virginia shook her head. "Wait until you feel better."

Listening to the Andrews women, Cody was drawn back to high school and all the time he'd spent with the family.

Rachel managed to get to her elbows, then went pale and closed her eyes. "I need to be the one to go. I know where Grandma kept her valuables."

The doctor put a hand on her shoulder and guided her back into a prone position before turning to the family. "Let's limit the number of visitors. Miss Andrews needs to rest."

An upbeat version of "Here Comes the Bride" started playing. All eyes went to Emily, who snatched her phone from her purse, swiped at the screen, and answered while stepping into the hallway.

A moment later, she returned. "The DJ's ten minutes out. Also, the caterer called and wanted to bring out some appetizers for us to taste." She patted Rachel's hand. "If you're sure you'll be okay, I'll take off. But if you need me to stay, I—"

"I'm fine. Go."

"I'll catch a ride back to the lodge with Emily and Justin so I can get Rachel's room ready," Virginia added.

Rachel again struggled to sit up. "Dad, my SUV is still at Grandma's. I need to get Timber's stuff."

"The dog," Virginia said slowly. "You want us to take the dog to our place?"

Everyone shot her a look, even Emily.

Virginia threw her hands into the air. "Okay, okay. It's only for a week. Timber's welcome."

Cody smiled. Growing up, Emily had wanted a cat but hadn't been willing to push for one. Rachel, he remembered, had pushed hard when she decided she wanted a dog. She'd put one on every Christmas list and often taped photos of puppies throughout the lodge, with the word *Please* written in marker.

Virginia had used the "We're too busy to have animals" argument throughout their childhood. In truth, the whole family, plus Cody, had known the girls' mother hated the idea of dealing with shedding hair and muddy paw prints on the floor.

"Chief Becker," Rachel pleaded, "let Dad get my SUV. Oh dear, I don't know where the keys are. Cody?"

"Don't worry. I have them." He pulled them from his pocket and handed them to Rachel's dad.

"I'd rather get you home, then fetch your vehicle," Dennis said.

"I'll bring her home, sir," Cody said. "I'll also stop by and get Timber from the vet."

Rachel's dad hesitated, then said, "All right. That way I can at least get a scope of the damage."

"I'll call my deputy and clear you to pick up her vehicle." Chief Becker pulled out his phone. "And I'll see if there's any news."

In the end, assured that Rachel was in no danger and indeed simply needed rest, the family dispersed.

"See you at home, honey," Dennis said. He hurried to catch up with Justin, who had opted to help with Rachel's vehicle rather than taste appetizers.

The doctor shot Cody and Chief Becker a reproachful glare. "Take it easy on her." Turning his attention to Rachel, he added, "Press the call button if you need anything, even if it's asking me to throw out stressful visitors." With that, he checked his watch and left the room.

Chief Becker pulled up a chair next to Rachel and said, "Good to see you. Town's boring without you driving snowmobiles into the river."

"That only happened once," Rachel protested weakly.

"And here you are, back in town, already on my radar." Chief Becker smiled and took out his tablet. "Nice to have you home." Shooting a glance at Cody, he said, "Both of you."

"Thank you, sir."

"Now," the chief began. "What time did you arrive at Nettie's cabin?"

"It was maybe five minutes after six."

"Tell me what happened." Chief Becker's fingers sailed across his tablet.

"I parked in the driveway. Timber was sitting on the passenger side. I came a day early because I wanted to get unpacked and, well, decompress without family drama. I got out of the car and took a few steps. I stood there for a bit, thinking about old times. Timber must have sensed something because he shoved past me. He always waits for my command, but he didn't this time. That's when part of the house exploded."

"Do you remember seeing any smoke? Before the explosion?" Cody asked.

Becker pinned Cody with a glare, then repeated the question, "Did you see smoke?"

"I didn't, but it was snowing hard, and"—she hesitated—"and I was crying."

Both men were quiet. Cody's heart ached at her admission.

"Okay, the house exploded, and then?" Becker encouraged.

"I hit the ground," Rachel continued. "Timber was next to me. I pulled him close and covered our heads to protect us from the debris flying everywhere. I stayed there for a few seconds, although it felt longer. Believe it or not, even lying there in the snow, I felt a wave of heat. Then, when the debris stopped falling, I got in the car and reached for my phone, but I had no service. I saw smoke and the hole in Grandma's house, but then Timber alerted."

"Alerted?"

"Timber's trained in search and rescue," Rachel said. With all that was going on, Cody had forgotten that Rachel was not only involved in search and rescue, but she ran a top training facility. No wonder she'd been so worried about her dog. Timber was more than a pet—he was a partner.

Cody could appreciate that. US Marshals usually worked with a partner. Since he was a Rolling Pine native and working undercover while in town for a wedding, his superiors had decided that he could work alone until he had firm evidence to prove Richard Hammonds—jewel thief and murderer—was working in the area. He could handle it, but he always preferred to work with a partner.

"And your dog noticed the man fleeing?" the chief asked.

"He did."

"What did you see?"

"Bulky black coat, one that fell almost to the knees. He was maybe your height, Chief, about five foot eleven. I believe he was left-handed."

"What makes you say that?" Cody asked.

"He carried his gun in his left hand."

"He had a gun?" Chief Becker leaned forward.

Cody could kick himself. Nothing about the scene he'd encountered had seemed normal. Not the car door being open, or Rachel's footprints in the snow, leading around to the back of the house instead of to the front door.

Chief Becker continued with his questions. "What kind of gun? Was it pointed at the ground, crooked in his arm, pointed at you?"

"Pointed at the ground," Rachel said. "It was too far away to see the details, but I own a gun myself"—she cited a brand and model commonly used by law enforcement—"and this was an inch or so bigger. He never aimed it at me."

Cody didn't know whether to be dismayed or relieved that Rachel owned a gun. "I didn't think to search for any other footprints once I found her. I wanted her safe and out of the cold."

Rachel met his gaze, her eyes warm.

Chief Becker stepped out the door, made a quick phone call, and came back. "You did everything right, but the gun complicates things. I wonder if Rachel disturbed a squatter who panicked when she pulled up in the driveway."

Cody didn't disagree with the chief's train of thought, but he did wish he'd scanned the perimeter as he scooped Rachel up and carried her to his car. He could blame it on the dog, who stayed at his feet, tensed for any indication that his mistress was in danger. He could blame it on the fear that had all but stopped his heart when he recognized Rachel. His training had melted away, and fierce protectiveness had surged through him.

"There were no footprints in front of the house. I saw no evidence that someone was inside," Rachel added.

"Since the property's backyard is the Arapahoe National Forest, it's possible the man exited from the rear. I'm going to go nose around." The chief stood, put on his hat, and tucked his tablet under his arm. "I'll head there now."

Cody changed from his seat against the wall to the one next to Rachel's bed. She didn't say anything, but she was clearly both annoyed and tired. He felt the same way.

He wished the doctor would return so he'd be free to follow the chief. Cody needed to talk with Becker about Hammonds.

Rachel muttered, "I should get to go with him. I'm the one who got knocked out."

"Good thing you're hardheaded," Cody teased. "Otherwise, that piece of house could have done some real damage." For now, he decided, she was his top priority. Everything else could wait.

"I don't understand. Debris had stopped falling," Rachel said, closing her eyes again, not quite masking her expression of pain. "If not, I wouldn't have run back there."

"Sometimes debris lodges in trees. Whatever hit you probably got caught in that old pine and happened to come loose the moment you were right under it." Cody knew it was too late to hunt for additional footprints. It had snowed steadily all morning. Plus, the firemen, deputy, and neighbors were trekking everywhere. Any remnant of evidence would have been stepped over, burnt, or melted.

What also bothered him was knowing that there was a slight chance the man Rachel had witnessed trekking across the snow was the very jewel thief Cody had come there to catch.

Maybe Richard Hammonds had figured out that Nettie's cabin was empty and had been hiding there.

It was a long shot, but if it was true, Rachel might be in danger because she'd seen him.

"*D*ad, I'm almost ready to go." Rachel balanced her cell phone on her shoulder—not an easy task even when her head wasn't spinning—as she signed a medical release form at the clinic's front desk later that afternoon.

"Justin and I are leaving the cabin. Half the town is here," her dad said. "The house doesn't look too bad from the outside, other than the destroyed corner. Justin managed to walk around back. He didn't see anything except debris."

Rachel smiled, thinking about how annoyed the chief would be with Justin. Still, the snow would have already covered up any footprints left by the intruder in the backyard, so it wasn't as if Justin had destroyed a crime scene. Her most fervent hope was that once Timber's paw healed enough to search, there'd still be a scent trail for him to follow.

And Timber had followed the man once, so he already knew his smell.

"I should be home in about thirty minutes," Rachel said.

Cody wrapped his coat around her and gathered the paperwork, then helped her to the door and opened it for her.

"I've called Chris," her dad continued. "He's going to meet us at the cabin as soon as they allow access. He can tell us the extent of the damage and repair cost for what I can't fix myself."

That was her father, the great fixer. Chris was the handyman who did all the work for the lodge, the big things her father couldn't do.

"Dad," Rachel said, ducking under Cody's arm as he held the door, "we're heading to Cody's Jeep. I'll call you if anything happens, okay?"

"Maybe I should swing by and pick you up. Cody can pick up Timber."

She wanted a hot bath, but there were more pressing things. "No, but thanks for the offer, Dad."

"Okay," her dad agreed, "see you when you get home." He ended the call.

There it was again, that word *home*. A mother to fuss over her and tell her that she needed to wear different shoes, ones that would keep her feet dry. A father to keep an eye on the tread on her tires and remind her to carry chains. A sister she used to stay up giggling and sharing secrets with.

She settled in the passenger seat and fastened her seat belt. "I'm ready".

He closed the door for her and hurried around to the driver's side. As they started down the street, she noted that Rolling Pine was ready for Christmas. An inflatable Santa waved from the window of Pinetop Hardware Store. A nativity scene braved the wind atop Fiona's Flower Shop. A few brave souls were out and about, bundled to ward off the cold and apparently oblivious to the freezing temperature. She didn't recognize anyone through the abundance of hats, scarves, and winter coats. At least a third of the coats were knee-length, black, and bulky, like that of the man she'd chased. That thought triggered another. "He wasn't carrying anything."

"What?"

"The man I tried to follow. Except for the gun, he didn't have anything in his hands, so he wasn't looting Grandma Nettie's house."

"That we know of," Cody said. "But he might have hightailed it out of there when he realized someone was there."

"True," Rachel agreed.

"If he'd found money, that would be easy enough to stash in a coat."

"I've been thinking about Grandma and her habits. I don't believe she ever felt the need to hide money. She trusted banks, and she didn't keep a lot of cash around as far as I know."

"What about other valuables? Something that would fit in a coat pocket?" Cody asked.

"She had some great old jewelry, mostly costume. Her favorite pieces were the ones my grandfather bought her when he was stationed in Arizona."

"Anything valuable?"

"No, Mom took most of it and had it priced. I think the most valuable piece was worth around $200."

At the end of the downtown district, Cody pulled into the parking area of the veterinary hospital. Cutouts of animals wearing Santa hats graced the front windows, and a sleigh with Christmas presents addressed to Watson, Beans, and Bear sat on the front porch.

Veterinarian Albert Levy worked out of an old farmhouse that the town had grown around. The living room had been converted into a reception area and the bedrooms into exam rooms.

Cody kept one hand under Rachel's arm and helped her through the door. She felt better but appreciated his solid assistance all the same. After checking in at the reception desk, Rachel moved from Cody's side to hug both the town librarian, Shelley David, who was there with her cat, and her third-grade teacher, Mr. Epstein, with his iguana. Before sitting down, Rachel reached out a hand to stroke the foot-long green reptile with a sprinkling of yellow on its spine. The iguana's enclosure had taken up a whole wall of Mr. Epstein's classroom when Rachel was a student.

"Celebrated his twelfth birthday last week," Mr. Epstein bragged as Dr. Levy entered the room, carrying a large crate with Timber asleep inside.

"He's still a little groggy I think," Dr. Levy said. "I've never cared for a more stoic dog. The cut was plenty deep and must have hurt."

Rachel stretched out her fingers to stroke the top of Timber's head through the grate. "That's my good boy," she whispered.

"There's not a shard left that I could feel, but I want him back in two days. I'll change the bandage then." He gestured to the dressing all the way up Timber's front left leg.

Dr. Levy handed her two prescriptions. "An antibiotic and some pain meds. Instructions are on the bottles. And I'm sorry to hear about Nettie's house."

Mr. Epstein chimed in, "I heard it was a small portion and will be easy to fix. You got lucky, especially interrupting a burglar."

"Someone broke into the library not too long ago," Shelley added. "Most of the books were open on the floor. It must have been kids. Nothing was taken, but I had to close for a week to get the books back on the shelves and in the right order."

"Did they steal your computers?" Cody asked.

"They didn't even touch the computers," Shelley said. "And they didn't take the petty cash either. Now that surprised me."

"Whoever is behind these break-ins, cash doesn't seem to be their objective," Dr. Levy said. "They tore through my barn and tossed it, but didn't take anything. Anything they could open, they did. Anything they could tip, they did. Saddle bags on the ground. Old jackets on top of that. They dumped feed. It's as if they were simply trying to make the biggest possible mess."

"Does the chief think it's kids?" Rachel asked.

"He hasn't said yet," Shelley added.

Dr. Levy shook his head. "It remains a mystery."

"And not the only one," Cody said.

Cody, already suspicious about the possible intruder at Nettie's cabin, added the library and Dr. Levy's barn to his mental list of places to investigate.

"Rachel, are you all right?" Dr. Levy asked.

The question jolted Cody, and he turned to see Rachel swaying a little. He caught her elbow, and she sent him a grateful smile. "I think we need to head out."

"Of course." Carrying Timber, Dr. Levy followed them to Cody's vehicle.

"Thanks, Dr. Levy," Rachel murmured.

A moment later she was in Cody's Jeep, leaning back in the passenger seat with her eyes closed while he secured Timber's crate in the back. "Thank you for everything. I'll be back to settle up tomorrow," he promised the veterinarian.

"I'm not worried about it," Dr. Levy said, heading back to the clinic. "Call me if Timber has any more problems."

Cody got behind the wheel and started the vehicle before reaching over to pat Rachel's arm. "Hey, you need to stay awake for a few more hours."

"I know."

"You hungry?" He slowly pulled out of the parking space, waiting for her answer.

She grimaced.

"Okay, I'll take you home," Cody said.

"No, I want to do a quick drive by Grandma Nettie's."

He hadn't thought it was a good idea at the clinic. He truly didn't think it was a good idea now. "You told your dad you'd be right home."

"I will be right home. Right after I see Grandma Nettie's house."

"Nothing's going to change between today and tomorrow. I'll keep an eye out."

"I won't be able to relax if I don't see it for myself."

Had she been any other witness to a crime or any other victim, he'd have driven her home and given instructions on what to expect next. But it was Rachel leaning back against his passenger seat. Her long dark hair curled around her neck, and her high cheekbones were a bit flushed.

Cody had always had a soft spot for Rachel. And when he'd finally realized that his feelings held the possibility of becoming something more, he had done what was right and broken up with her sister. But he'd never worked up the courage to ask if Rachel might have felt the same way.

"I need to—" Her phone buzzed before she could finish. She fished it from her purse and answered it. "Hi, Mom."

For the next few minutes he listened as she firmly told her mother that she'd be going to Nettie's and that everything was fine. Then she put the phone on speaker, saying, "Mom wants to talk to you."

"Cody, I think you should bring Rachel home," Virginia said.

Silently, he agreed, but Rachel shook her head.

"Cody?" Rachel's mother pressed.

Cody had a choice. He could take Rachel home and be in her mother's good graces. Or he could take Rachel to Nettie's house and be in Rachel's good graces. He opted for making Rachel happy. "Twenty minutes max. Then I'll bring her straight home."

"But—"

"Mom," Rachel interrupted. "We're already on Grandma's street."

Virginia sighed. "Twenty minutes."

Clearly exasperated, Rachel ended the call and stared out the window at Nettie's house. It had been cordoned off.

"At least they've covered the damage with a tarp," Rachel observed as they rolled past. "It's not nearly as bad as I thought it would be. The explosion felt as if it should have leveled the whole house."

Cody parked in front of his parents' house, which was a short way down the street from Nettie's. Getting out, he circled the Jeep and opened Rachel's door. She was still flushed, but the pinched groove between her eyes had disappeared, and her color was better.

Cody had barely helped Rachel from the vehicle before his mother hurried out from the house, carrying one of his dad's old coats.

"Hi, honey."

"Hi, Mom." Cody hugged her, then shrugged into the coat. "Rachel, why don't you stay with my mom while I go check out the damage?"

"No way," Rachel said.

Cody could tell she was trying to speak firmly, but since she was still nursing a headache, it came out more like a whimper. Then he noted something he'd missed that morning in all the excitement. The Barnhart house next to Nettie's was for sale. Virginia Andrews's photo and phone number were listed on the yard sign.

"When did the Barnharts decide to move?" Cody asked.

"A month ago. They're going to Arizona. Scottsdale, actually, so they'll be Rachel's neighbors." Cody's mom smiled at Rachel. "Come on in. I'd love to catch up. How are you feeling?"

"I'm feeling better, and thank you, Rose. I promise we can catch up later. For now I'm going to stick with Cody. I want to know what's going on at my grandmother's house."

"Chris Mack says you got off easy. You'll need a new bathroom and part of the hallway."

"When did you talk to Chris?" Rachel asked.

"He was here about thirty minutes ago. The police wouldn't let him get close." His mother moved toward Cody's Jeep and peered in at the back seat. "What a gorgeous dog. Probably tired from everything that happened, isn't he?"

"Yes, but he'll come around soon," Rachel said.

"Do you need some water for him?"

"Not right now, but thank you again," Rachel said.

"Mom, has anyone else stopped by Nettie's house?" Cody asked.

"What do you mean?"

"Gawkers? Curiosity seekers?"

"There have been a few," his mom said. "Bob Lewis and Biggles. They came with the new owner of the Pine Place Motel, who bought the place about two years ago. His wife died of cancer a few months ago and I get the sense that he's a little lost. He has adult kids, but I don't think they come to visit much." She gave Cody a look that implied he was in danger of falling into the same category. "I also saw the young couple who opened a coffee house on Main next to the hardware store. The baked goods there are wonderful. Speaking of treats, I made your favorite brownies."

Before Cody could ask any more questions, his phone sounded. He took it from his pocket and recognized the number. "Hello, Virginia."

Five minutes later, Rachel grumbled as she adjusted her seat belt. "I can't believe my mother called you at the twenty-minute mark."

"Some things never change," Cody said.

"If only that were true," she murmured, staring out the window.

4

They hadn't gone a block before Cody remembered the doctor's instruction to take it easy on Rachel. So far, Cody had failed miserably. He would do better.

"Emily seems well," he said.

"She must be excited about the wedding," Rachel said.

Cody knew, as did everyone in town, that the sisters had been at odds for six years. Rachel had brought a college boyfriend home to meet her family, and the next thing everyone knew, Emily and Tyler had married. A short year into their marriage, Tyler was killed in a car accident.

According to Cody's mother, Rachel had been understandably devastated by Tyler and Emily's wedding but had handled it gracefully, even serving as her sister's maid-of-honor. His heart ached, thinking how Rachel must have felt going through such an ordeal.

"It was kind of strange being in the emergency clinic again," Cody mused out loud, hoping to get Rachel talking. "We spent enough time there when we were in high school, didn't we?"

Her eyes were closed when he glanced over, but she smiled and said, "You broke your nose playing football."

"And you broke your leg sliding into second base."

"Yeah, but I was safe."

He chuckled. "I guess. Not that it did much good since I had to carry you off the field and drive you to the clinic."

Rolling Pine had been a great place to grow up. Much of the winter was spent snowmobiling and skiing. Then, they'd all worked summers at Rolling Pine's White-Water Rafting Adventures theme park. While Emily clerked in the store, he and Rachel had served as raft guides. Sometimes he thought the routine of hauling those rafts and loading them up with people—some without a shred of fear and others terrified but determined to have an adventure anyway—was more of a workout than he'd done in boot camp.

Rachel peered at him. "What are you smiling at?"

"Memories. I miss Rolling Pine," Cody admitted. "I miss your family. And you." His tone grew serious as he thought of the past, of mistakes made and time lost, of the feelings he wished he'd had the courage to confess to her.

Was it too late?

He had been so young and uncertain. When his and Emily's dating relationship became more and more like a friendship than a romance, it had been starkly different from the way he'd grown to feel about Rachel. He later realized she had been the right one for him all along. "For so long, I thought you would end up being my sister-in-law."

"Yeah, I thought that too," Rachel said, closing her eyes once more.

There were so many memories that he struggled to choose one that might keep her alert and smiling. "Do you remember my eighteenth birthday?"

Rachel winced. "You were mad at Emily."

"Of course I was. We were a month shy of graduating from high school, it was my birthday, and she'd promised to zip-line in Breckenridge with me."

"She was never a daredevil like you were," Rachel reminded him. "Emily had a great time going through all the tourist shops while she waited for us. And I had a great time zip-lining in her place. I'd go again in a heartbeat. I always felt bad that you wound up dragging me along so often. Mom always figured I was the perfect chaperone, but really,

I wanted to hang out with my sister and—and you."

Cody's fingers gripped the steering wheel as he pulled into the Rocky Mountains Lodge parking lot. Rachel was obviously exhausted, and he didn't feel like talking about old times any longer, because the twinge of regret over all the things he wanted to tell her was too much to bear.

If Rachel thought that her headache would diminish the tug on her heart when she caught sight of the Rocky Mountains Lodge, she was mistaken. Despite the pain and pressure lingering at her temples, she wanted to run through the doors shouting that she was finally home.

The same Santa and elves decorations that had skied down the side of the lodge for the last twenty Christmases greeted Rachel. The giant pine to the left of the parking lot sparkled with hundreds of lights. The piled-up snow might be new, but she'd climbed to the top of many a mound when she was younger, feeling like the queen of the world.

More than ever, Rachel knew she had to find a way to bury the strife between her and Emily and start looking to the future instead of the past.

"I'll get Timber," Cody said, exiting the Jeep and coming to the passenger side to help Rachel out.

She began to protest, even though she secretly enjoyed his attention. He had seemed pensive in the car while talking about old times, and she wondered if any of his thoughts mirrored hers. Rachel had always felt a tug of chemistry between her and Cody, but she would never have come between him and Emily by admitting her feelings. Over time, she had wished away those inklings of affection, but matters of the heart weren't that simple.

While Cody lifted Timber's crate from the back of his Jeep, Rachel carefully maneuvered between the snow, slush, and sand dotting the parking lot. Leaning heavily on the handrail, she trod carefully up the steps and onto the large front porch.

"Are you going to make it?" Cody asked from behind her. He held Timber's crate in a firm grip.

"Yes, but I am really tired."

"And you still have a headache." He pushed open the door and a wall of warmth hit her face, banishing the icy chill of winter that had followed them in.

"Rachel," Kristin Fairchild, the manager of Rocky Mountains Lodge and Emily's best friend, called across the foyer. She beamed at the lodge's customers who milled around the large, comfortable room. "We have a big wedding here Saturday, and this is the bride's sister and maid of honor."

A young couple checking in at the front desk glanced toward Rachel and smiled. Rachel stamped the snow off her shoes and waved a greeting as Cody guided her across the lobby to the ornate door that led into her parents' living area.

A green wreath with berries, tiny gift boxes, and photos of every family member hung on the door. Cody tried the knob, discovered it was unlocked, and pushed it open. Once in the living room, he cast about for the best place to set Timber's crate.

"Do you remember where Rachel's bedroom is, Cody?" Rachel's mother emerged from the kitchen, wiping her hands on a dish towel. "You can put the dog in there."

Rachel took a moment to reach through the crate's openings, lightly stroking her dog's brow. Timber, jostled awake by the trip from the car to the lodge and intrigued by all the new scents and sights, tried to stand but couldn't quite do it while Cody balanced his crate in the air.

"Cody, would you mind taking him outside for a moment?"

"No problem." Cody disappeared with the crate down the hall to the back door.

"I'll get an old towel, and wipe Timber's paws when he comes back inside," Rachel assured her mother.

"No, I'll hand Cody a towel and he can do it. You sit and rest." Virginia was gone before Rachel could protest.

Rachel had no other choice but to obey, curling up on the big chair in the front of the fireplace. Eyes closed, she listened as her mother bustled about, picking things up and setting them back down, straightening furniture. After a moment, she heard the back door open and close, followed by Cody saying, "Good dog."

"I've got a towel." Virginia hurried down the hall before Cody could get too far inside the hallway.

When her mother and Cody returned to the living room, Rachel forced her eyes open. "Is Timber okay?"

"He's back in the crate in your old room, resting. Smart dog. He was a bit wobbly but very careful of his foot."

"There are some appetizers left from the taste testing," her mother said. "Are you two hungry?"

Cody checked his watch. "I need to get going. I have some things I need to take care of."

Rachel shrugged out of his jacket and held it out toward him. Until then, she'd forgotten she'd been wearing it. She smiled at the memory of Cody's mother hustling out to give him one of his dad's old coats. Rachel's mind had been so fuzzy, she hadn't even realized what was going on.

"You don't need it?" he asked.

"She has two hanging in her closet," her mom said. "And there are at least a dozen she can use in lost and found. It's amazing to me that people can walk off and leave behind perfectly good winter coats."

Cody touched Rachel's shoulder. "Take care, and call me if you need me."

"Tell your mother I said hello," Rachel's mom said to him, then turned to her daughter. "Rachel, your bed is made up for you. I'll get you a glass of water and then you can rest."

Rachel followed her mother into her childhood bedroom. Except for the bed, dresser, suitcases, and dog crate, nothing belonged to her personally. After she'd graduated from college and moved to Arizona, her mother had transformed the room into a combination guest room and sewing room.

Rachel's mother had a bucket list. Learning to sew was around ninth on the list if Rachel remembered correctly. Becoming a grandmother was currently first.

"You feel all right? Need anything? I can—"

"I'm fine, Mom. I'll take a hot shower and lie down for a while. Then I'll join you for supper."

Her mother hesitated as if she wanted to say something more. Then she pursed her lips and left.

Rachel sat on the edge of the bed, finally alone. *What a day.* Exhaustion, which had hovered around her like a fog, seeped into her bones. Forgoing the shower for the moment, she decided to crawl under the covers and try to sleep. She opened her suitcase and fished out a nightshirt. After changing out of her sweater and jeans, Rachel folded the clothes, pausing when her hand touched something hard in the pants pocket. Carefully, she pulled out a gold necklace with a tangled chain. She'd completely forgotten about it.

Her necklace from her grandmother's house seemed unaffected by the explosion. Rubbing her fingers over the piece, Rachel tried to picture Nettie wearing it, but couldn't. It was way too delicate, whereas

Grandma Nettie had favored chunky jewelry, with the exception of her wedding ring.

Rachel examined the small, diamond-like stones and guessed that they were probably cubic zirconia. The biggest stone, however, didn't look quite right. After a moment spent untangling the chain, Rachel held up a single gold earring. The stone she'd originally thought part of the necklace was at the top, on the end of the stud. Three strands of tiny pear-shaped gems dangled from it—probably more cubic zirconia.

Rachel set the two pieces on the dresser and finished changing into her nightshirt. She'd ask her mother about the jewelry later. Before crawling into bed, she knelt next to Timber. To her relief, his black and brown chest rose and fell easily. She'd sleep better knowing he was all right. And she really wanted to sleep.

The bed linens smelled of lavender, and the pillows had been plumped. Through the walls she could hear faint traces of her father's favorite country music station, as well as the other familiar sounds and aromas that had lulled her to sleep throughout her childhood.

Closing her eyes, she felt the day's events start to drift away. She was on the verge of drifting off when she realized something.

The earring had been for pierced ears.

But Grandma Nettie hadn't had pierced ears—she always wore clip-ons.

Too exhausted to muse over the information for more than a few seconds, Rachel felt her eyelids begin to grow heavy again, and the thought slipped away as sleep claimed her.

After leaving the Rocky Mountains Lodge, Cody headed home for a shower and to see if he'd received any updates on the jewel-thief case. He hadn't, but his superior wanted Cody to check in. Cody doubted that a report about an exploding cabin, a mysterious fleeing suspect, and caring for a wounded woman and dog was what his supervisor had in mind.

After he made the call, Cody's mother served a dinner of salad, spaghetti, and garlic bread. With his father out of town, she was happy for her son's company and wanted details about the explosion and the Andrews family.

"They think the water heater exploded," Cody said.

"That happened to the church secretary a few years back. The heater rocketed into the sky and landed on her back porch. Good thing they weren't home. Maybe your dad should check out our water heater?"

"It's a good idea." Cody pinched off a bite of garlic bread. "Mom, have you seen anyone suspicious walking around Nettie's place, or in the neighborhood? Someone who doesn't belong there?"

"We've had some extra traffic since the Barnharts' house went up for sale, but no one has put in an offer yet. If you want to know my opinion, I think they're asking too much."

"What about a single male, maybe a snowshoer?"

"Why?"

Cody didn't hesitate. Chief Becker would likely arrive tomorrow to ask the same questions. "Rachel saw a man hurrying away from the house after the explosion, across Nettie's backyard."

His mother frowned in concentration. "You know, I get used to seeing strangers exploring the forest. I can't say anyone has stood out lately or made me suspicious."

Cody cleared the table, then washed the dishes and placed them in the drainer. He begged off watching television with his mother and once again put on his snow gear. As he walked out the door, he switched on the Christmas lights, knowing his mom would like that, then he got in his Jeep and headed for town. A quick phone call to the police station gave him the information he needed.

Late evening diners filled every booth and table at the Pine Derby Restaurant. Cody stepped into the familiar haunt from his teenage years and scanned the crowd until he spotted Chief Becker downing a burger and fries at the back. Sliding in across from the man, Cody said, "Mind if I join you?"

"Not a bit. I've been expecting you."

Checking to make sure no one was paying attention, Cody pulled out his badge and slid it across the table.

Becker studied the emblem and raised an eyebrow. "US Marshal, eh? Wasn't expecting that. Where's your horse?"

"Probably the same place you keep yours." Cody pocketed his badge.

Becker laughed. "Okay, I deserved that. I take it you're not here solely for Emily's wedding."

"I completed training last year, so for the most part I've been sitting in courtrooms, escorting prisoners, and acting as a bodyguard should a politician need one. That all changed when I requested a week off to visit family and attend Emily's wedding."

"How so?" Becker asked between bites of burger.

"I was invited to join a special task force. Last month, we received an anonymous tip that Rolling Pine is the potential location of a fugitive known to us as Richard Hammonds."

Becker stopped eating.

"Hammonds is a jewel thief who's been known to kill to get what he wants." Cody pulled a tablet from a pocket inside his coat, tapped in his password, and handed his device to the chief.

Becker read the case files in silence. Finally, he prompted, "You said he's 'known to you' as Richard Hammonds?"

"It's the name we associated with the first burglary. We don't believe it's his real name."

"The name doesn't ring a bell. Do you have any photos?"

Cody took back the tablet, opened a new screen, and returned it to the chief. "Every photo we have is dark and grainy, usually from low-resolution video surveillance. We don't have a lot of particulars, but we're sure that he's slightly under six feet, slender, between the ages of thirty and forty-five, white—"

"You've just described half the male population of Rolling Pine."

"I know," Cody said. "I've described someone similar to me. And you, for that matter."

Becker laughed. "Believe me, forty-five is in my rearview mirror."

"Our best images so far are from an airport Hammonds passed through. And as far as behavior goes, based on his history, we know that Hammonds prefers to work residential areas."

"Really? Why?"

"Stealing from neighbors rather than from retailers with fancy alarm systems makes it easier to stay under the radar and keep from getting caught."

"Video cameras are everywhere, and a lot of homes have security systems now."

Cody nodded. "We're pretty sure that before he makes a move, he plans out a way to avoid them."

"And you think he's in Rolling Pine? Is his mark a townie, or perhaps a winter visitor?"

"We don't know. Whoever left the tip said Hammonds has been here a while. One thing we do know is that for almost eighty percent of the victims, it's not a random heist. Hammonds manages to learn their habits so he knows for certain where the jewels are, the best time to steal them, and how to leave without a trace."

"Inside help could include delivery drivers, caterers, hotel maintenance staff, and any number of other people," Chief Becker said.

"Exactly."

The chief considered in silence for a few seconds. "Off the top of my head, I can think of three families that might have jewelry in the ballpark of what your guy goes after. Do you want me to touch base with them?"

"No. Please send me their information via email and let me do it. I don't want them to start acting suspicious and scare our guy off."

"But he's already killed—"

"Let me handle some preliminary work first, and if there's even a hint of risk, I'll alert the families."

"All right," Chief Becker said. "We definitely draw tourists that are wealthy, but do they bring their valuables with them to ski? I doubt it. Have you spoken to Dennis Andrews or any other motels' or hotels' management about this?"

"I will. I arrived this morning, and right away I got caught up with Rachel and the explosion. Has your station received reports of any jewelry stolen lately?"

"In the last year? Or beyond that?"

"A bit beyond."

"Watches," Chief Becker said. "We had a summer visitor two years ago—someone stole his Rolex, worth about twenty thousand dollars. Found out it was his son who pawned it for considerably less than it was worth."

Cody took a small notebook from his pocket. "Which pawn shop?"

"Second Chance, over in Cedar City."

"Anything other than watches?" Cody asked.

"Shelley David had a watch go missing about two years ago. Bob Lewis gave it to her as a thank-you for something she did. Couldn't have been worth much. She'd done a story hour at the library and read the kids a book about telling time. Shelley took it off, passed it around, and then set the watch on a shelf. When she went back a few hours later, it was gone. She figured one of the children took it. The main reason she reported it missing was so that Bob would know how much she regretted losing it."

Cody tapped his pen against the table. "Hammonds's smallest take was $450,000 back in Detroit, Michigan, six years ago. His MO seems to be about every two years. As far as we can tell, over the last twelve years, he's hit every twenty-two to twenty-six months. But four years ago, he skipped a cycle."

"You might have a crime that went unreported."

"That's what we believe."

"So, you have at least five or six verified burglaries where he's averaged how much profit?"

"Between fifty thousand dollars and half a million, give or take."

Becker whistled, pushed his plate to the side, and leaned forward. "So, my experience with the US Marshals is that a whole team of you swoop in, spread out, and catch your guy. How many agents should I expect in the area?"

"Just me for now. Like I said, we received an anonymous tip. We're not willing to shake the tree until we have more to go on."

A waitress came and took Cody's order of coffee and hot apple pie.

After she left, Becker said, "I'm surprised the Marshals are putting so much credence into one anonymous tip."

"We've tracked every hit. He goes where the wealthy go, and the wealthy like to ski. The tip tracks with Hammonds's past behavior."

"I still say you don't need to bring a million dollars in jewels on your ski trip."

Cody nodded in agreement. "But on the off chance the tip is good, I'm here anyway for Emily's wedding. If I find any proof that Hammonds is active in the area, well, it will be worth it."

"I can live without so much action in my small town," Becker said. "Who needs that much money?"

"Our profiler says it's one of two things. It's either as much a game as a moneymaker, or Hammonds has huge expenditures and steals to meet his obligations."

"Could he be a gambler?" Becker asked.

"If he is, the game is so deep we can't track him."

"With the dark web, that's possible."

"Yes, and he's smart. We can't find where he's fenced the jewelry. We figure a private collector, but we've only reclaimed three pieces. One necklace was sold at a garage sale, believe it or not. The man who bought it took it to a consignment store and by the time we tracked it back and knocked on the garage seller's door, he'd passed away. Every lead evaporates before we gain any traction."

"Frustrating," Becker said. "Still, I'm surprised this is on the US Marshals' slate. You guys tend to go after the truly dangerous fugitives."

"Oh, he's plenty dangerous. His last burglary had casualties. A Dallas woman and her son walked in on a burglary in progress."

Cody opened another screen on his tablet and handed it back to Becker. To a typical viewer, the image on the screen was a crime scene like any other that might appear on a segment of the five o'clock news. "We kept one important detail from the press."

Becker studied the photo. "No sign of a struggle."

"You got it. We're convinced the Chapmans walked in on him, but based on evidence—or should I say lack thereof—we're pretty sure they knew and trusted their killer."

"Honey?"

Rachel heard the word, recognized her mother's voice, and tried to open her eyes.

"Breakfast is ready and everyone's at the table."

Taking a breath, Rachel rolled over too quickly, then had to wait until a wave of headache pain and nausea subsided.

Timber whined.

"I think your dog needs attention." Her mother sounded worried. "Do you think he'll let me take him out? I'll get my coat."

Rachel groaned. "I got it, Mom."

"Okay." Her mother tiptoed from the room.

Rachel slid out of bed. Except for exhaustion and headache, she felt okay. Gingerly, she shrugged into her coat and found an old pair of boots in the closet.

Timber barked and moved toward the crate door, obviously feeling better.

"Coming, buddy." Rachel slipped into her boots, opened the crate, and stepped into the hallway with Timber following. She could hear Emily's voice and her dad's laughter coming from the kitchen. Rachel turned a corner and ran into something—or rather someone.

"Hey." Emily's fiancé, Justin Fletcher, laughed and backed up a little.

Timber barked but quickly settled down at Rachel's sign.

"Beautiful dog," he observed.

"You like dogs?"

"I do." Justin patted Timber's head, and because Rachel had given the sign, Timber allowed it. It gave Rachel a moment to study the man who would be her brother-in-law by the end of the week. Except for the day before at the clinic, it was her first time meeting him in person. After he'd proposed, she'd congratulated Justin and Emily via video chat, but that had been their only contact.

Justin Fletcher was tall and lanky, with floppy dark brown hair just touching his shoulders. "You're looking better."

"I feel much better. Thank you for fetching my car and bringing in my luggage."

"I wish I could have done more." Justin moved aside, letting her pass.

The cold hit her the minute she stepped out the back door and her boots sank into the snow. Although he limped a bit, Timber didn't seem bothered by the temperature. He glanced toward Rachel for permission to explore, and after her brief nod, sniffed around for a few minutes, investigated the yard, and then came back to her side. She ordered him to stay at the doorway, fetched a towel, and dried him off as best she could before taking him back to her room. Not having to worry about Timber bothering her mother was another reason Rachel had wanted to stay at Grandma Nettie's cabin rather than the lodge.

"Hope you're hungry for pancakes." Her father held up a spatula when she joined them in the kitchen. "A lot or a little?"

"Let's start with a little."

A few minutes later, he put a fluffy, steaming pancake on a plate and set it in front of her.

Emily pushed the syrup to her. "Are you feeling any better?"

"Much. I'll take a shower after breakfast, change into clean clothes, and be ready to go."

"I scheduled your dress fitting for today, but we can push it back if you need to," Emily said.

"I think I can handle it."

"Good, and we're having lunch after." Emily passed Rachel a piece of paper as Kristin came into the kitchen.

Kristin, Emily's friend, and manager of the lodge, had long been considered a third daughter, especially after living with the Andrewses when her parents moved to Denver during her and Emily's senior year. She put the remaining two pancakes on a plate and pulled up a spare chair to sit beside Rachel. Kristin pointed to the paper Rachel held and said, "I see you have your itinerary. I'm yellow."

"I was about to explain," Emily said. "It's color coded. Rachel, you're green. Cross out anything you don't feel comfortable doing and let me know. I'll either reschedule it for later this week or find a way around it."

"I have one of those too." Justin held up his itinerary, which featured blue highlights.

Rachel's dad joked, "My piece of paper is my checkbook."

"Daddy," Emily protested.

"I'm chipping in too," Justin told Rachel, giving Emily a smile that belonged in a romantic movie.

Rachel's opinion of her sister's fiancé went up a notch. "I don't think Emily's mentioned what you do for a living."

"I guess you could call me an entrepreneur. I graduated with a degree in finance, and I invest in small businesses."

"And you came to Rolling Pine to invest in a business?" Rachel asked.

Justin shook his head. "I was actually checking out land acquisitions. During ski season, lodging in Aspen and Vail is booked months, sometimes as much as a year, in advance." He sent Rachel's dad an apologetic glance. "I was thinking of giving your family a little competition."

"And now?" Rachel asked. Her stomach felt a bit funny. Her father's biggest worry had always been land developers and investors. Was her sister really going to marry one?

"Once I met Emily," Justin said, "it was over. I'm getting my real estate license online."

"He'll work with me at Andrews Realty," Rachel's mother said. "I always hoped one of you girls would."

Emily broke in. "There's a chance that eventually Justin and I will build a slightly bigger lodge adjacent to this one, and run it ourselves."

"With all the short-term rental opportunities, I'm also thinking about buying and flipping some of the older homes in town," Justin added.

"As investments," Rachel filled in for him, noting that everyone but Kristin and her father looked pleased. Dad didn't like change much, especially if it altered anything about Rolling Pine. Rachel didn't know why Kristin wasn't impressed.

Justin must have picked up on the slight tension because he changed the subject. "Emily's told me about you and your dog participating in search and rescue. How long have you been doing that?"

"I've been handling canines for three years now and have built a pretty solid reputation."

"So that's all you do? Work with dogs?" Justin asked.

Rachel bristled. "Most of my work is with both dogs and their humans. I also run a boarding kennel where people leave their dogs with me when they are on vacation."

"Which makes the most money? Sorry, but as an investor, I'm curious."

Surprised by the question, Rachel hesitated before responding. "I would say the boarding."

"But search and rescue is where your heart lies," her father chimed in.

"It is."

"Tell me your scariest adventure while you were out on a search and rescue." Justin seemed genuinely interested.

"The scariest was hunting down a human smuggler the police believed had killed a man."

"And you caught him?" Justin asked.

"Timber did. The criminal must have been scared of dogs. I've never seen anyone try to climb a cactus before, but this man did."

"What's your favorite part of search and rescue?" Justin took his plate, gathered everyone else's, and headed for the sink.

"Finding lost children alive. No question."

"Does that happen often?"

"It does," Rachel's mother said. "Rachel's had her name in the papers four times."

"Mom, are you keeping tabs on me?" Rachel smiled. Her mother rarely asked about her work, usually focusing on the lodge and always mentioning that they could use Rachel around to help keep it running. Rachel always interpreted that to mean her mother missed her and wished she were home.

"Of course I do. Not only keeping tabs on you, but also worrying about you, especially when you're trying to rescue people after flash floods."

"Sounds dangerous," Justin said.

"It can be. Most of the time, though, I'm searching for lost hikers or kids."

Justin stayed at the sink and picked up a dishcloth but didn't turn on the water. "I've read that all it takes is for the dog to smell an item of clothing or something like that, and then they can find nearly anything. How does that work?"

"It's not always that simple," Rachel said. "When we're called in, we need to be at the spot where the missing person was last seen.

Then Timber follows a trail of mostly flesh particles."

"By sniffing the air?"

"Some dogs do that. Timber's a tracker, as opposed to an air-scent dog. Air-scent dogs can find any human in the vicinity."

"Why didn't you train him to be an air-scent dog?" Kristin asked.

"Timber was the first dog I trained, and I wasn't confident yet. When my team is called up, the dogs I've helped train since Timber include more advanced trackers, as well as air-scent dogs."

Justin still made no move to begin washing dishes. "Have you found many dead bodies? I think that would be the hardest part of your job."

"It's why I'm glad Timber's a tracker and not an air-scent dog. Most cadaver dogs are air-scent."

On that note, her mother stood up, started gathering the condiments, and said brightly, "We have a lot to do today."

Emily spoke up. "Mom, do you think we can find time to drive to Aspen after lunch? I need a few things, and there's not enough time to order them online."

"We can do that. I took this whole week off work." Rachel's mom finished clearing the table.

Justin leisurely started doing dishes and Rachel's father opened the paper.

"Rachel, do you need me at the fitting today?" Emily asked. "If so, I'll rearrange my schedule. If not, Kristin said she'd go with you."

"I can go by myself."

"I need to try on my dress too," Kristin said. "When I tried it on two weeks ago, it was too big. They've made some alterations."

"Great," Emily said. "We'll meet for lunch after. It will be fun. And, Rachel, I'm so glad you're home."

According to the itinerary, the fitting was at ten o'clock, giving Rachel about an hour to unpack and shower. She headed for her room.

First, she spread yesterday's paper on the floor and set Timber's food and water dish on it. Timber drank a little and lay down. "I promise, we'll go for a walk as soon as I get my list completed."

Carefully, she put away her clothes, making sure to close each drawer. She'd learned young that an open drawer was an invitation for one of the cleaning staff to organize her things. Then she made sure her suitcases were snapped shut before shoving them under the bed.

Finally, she hopped in the shower. Feeling much better afterward, she dried her hair and dressed in jeans and a red cowl-neck sweater. She found thick socks still in the dresser and glanced in the mirror once more.

Not bad. She almost felt like herself again.

Her eyes fell on her grandmother's single earring and necklace, resting on the dresser where she'd placed them after finding them in her pocket the day before.

Rachel unclasped the necklace and put it on. Impressed, she noted how the round diamonds caught the light. It might not have been Grandma Nettie's taste, but it sure was classic. Too bad she didn't have the second earring.

*M*onday morning, staring out of his parents' front window, Cody saw gray weather and side drifts caused by an early snowplow. It was a good thing the basement still had the workout station he and his brother, Todd, had put together when they were in high school. After working up a sweat, Cody felt a little better.

Following a shower, Cody spent some time setting up an old table, finding a comfortable chair, and hanging two corkboards. His parents' printer was too old and slow for his needs, so shortly after ten, Cody headed into town. He would purchase a new printer and leave it for his parents' use.

Rolling Pine in December was mostly populated by locals, many of whom were likely at work. The tourists were skiing in Aspen. The Pining for Joe coffee place was full of retirees, plus a handful of young people with laptops open and fingers flying across the keyboards. Cody was happy to pay more for coffee than he usually would if it meant learning something about the new-to-town people his mother had noticed lurking around after the explosion at Rachel's grandmother's house.

Of course, Richard Hammonds would probably not fake finding a wife, buying a business, and working start-up hours, so the young couple who owned the coffee shop were probably a dead end. Still, it wouldn't hurt to talk to them.

After waiting in line, Cody stepped up to the glass display case, ordered an apple fritter and a large dark-roast coffee, and started a conversation with the redheaded woman filling his request. "Are you the owner?"

"I am. My name is Kate Welch." The woman smiled and wrapped his fritter in waxed paper before popping it into a brown bag and adding a napkin. "My husband, Stuart, is co-owner."

"My mother is Rose Scott. She says you make wonderful baked goods, so I'm excited to try the apple fritter."

"We love your mother. She comes in two or three times a week and has mentioned how much you love brownies. I'll throw in a complimentary one and let you decide which is better—the brownie or the fritter."

"That would be great. Thanks." He studied the space. "If I remember correctly, this used to be a store selling T-shirts and such."

"It was my uncle's place. When he died, he left it to my mother. She was ready to sell, but when Stuart and I came down to help pack up my uncle's home, we fell in love with the town and decided to start a business here. We were both working for a big coffee chain, so we had an idea of how to run a shop of our own. So far, it's working."

"She's right." A cheerful-looking young man set a steaming mug of coffee on the counter. "I'm Stuart, by the way. Can we get you anything else?"

"Cody Scott. Nice to meet you. I think I'm all set." Cody moved to a seat by the window. He took out his tablet while nibbling on the fritter and sipping his coffee. After half an hour, Cody could tell that the husband-and-wife team ran the place themselves, and his stakeout wasn't likely to turn up any new-to-town employees who might secretly be jewel thieves.

He searched online for the other recent arrival his mother had mentioned—the owner of the Pine Place Motel. His mom was right. Burt Michaels had bought the old motel two years before and was in the process of renovating while renting out the rooms. Cody didn't figure Michaels for a suspect, primarily because he was over sixty—too old to fit Hammonds's profile. Besides, when Richard Hammonds was in Dallas helping himself to the Chapmans' wealth and committing murder, Michaels had been negotiating a deal for the run-down Pine Place Motel. Still, a visit to Michaels wouldn't hurt. Maybe Michaels had checked in a single male guest who didn't fit the profile of a typical tourist.

Cody slid the remnants of the fritter back into the bag with the brownie, then grabbed his coffee. Right before noon, he stepped out of a downtown department store with a new printer and watched as Justin Fletcher led the Andrews clan into the Pine Derby Restaurant.

Standing by his Jeep, Cody weighed his options—head home and get to work, or stop for lunch with old friends? He stuck the printer in the back seat and then hurried to the restaurant.

Bill Querty, whose family owned the restaurant and who had been one of Cody's high school friends, held the door for him. "Heard you were back."

"Barely twenty-four hours," Cody said, holding out his hand.

Bill shook it vigorously with a grin. "Ah, you know small towns. Your mother called my mother. How are you doing?"

"Can't complain. Mind if I join the Andrews party?"

Bill led Cody to the Andrewses' table, where they welcomed him with enthusiasm. Cody took a seat next to Emily and asked Rachel, "How are you feeling today?"

"I have a bit of a headache, but it's nothing I can't handle."

"Cody, I'm so glad you're here," Emily gushed. "You have to see the bridesmaids' dresses." She handed him her phone, and he scrolled through several photos of Rachel and Kristin in long dresses.

Cody remembered that at Emily's first wedding, there had been a small army walking down the aisle. He had sat in the center of the church next to his parents and siblings, feeling a little relieved that he wasn't the groom. He still cared about Emily as if she were a sibling, but anything more between them wasn't meant to be.

Especially not when his heart was drawn to Rachel.

"It's the first time for me," Justin put in. "I'd just as soon have eloped, but Emily wouldn't hear of it."

"No indeed." Turning to Cody, Emily said, "Justin's brother, the best man, should be here Friday morning."

"He's in South Africa," Justin explained. "He's flying in Friday and renting a car, and will be here in time for the rehearsal."

The waitress came and took their drink orders. Cody watched the engaged couple interact and thought about his own dating life. For some reason, he hadn't met anyone he cared enough about to take out past the third or fourth date, partly because of work but mostly because of lack of interest. He knew his heart belonged to Rachel, but the timing had never been right, and she always seemed out of reach.

"This has been one of our coldest winters," Virginia said across the table from Cody. "We'll need to hire an extra valet to handle coats and such."

The waitress returned with their drinks and took their lunch orders. Cody leaned back and studied the table. Justin paid more attention to his cell phone than to Emily, but she didn't object, as she was going over last-minute details with her sister and mother. Kristin stared out the window, uncharacteristically quiet.

Cody remembered with a jolt that Kristin's fiancé, George, had gone missing four years ago. Helping to plan her best friend's wedding couldn't be easy.

"Okay," Emily said. "Venue, check. Food, check. Minister, check. Attendants, check. Flowers, check. Oh—how could I have forgotten? Something old, something new, something borrowed, something blue."

"You have plenty of blue," Virginia said.

"And plenty of new," Kristin added.

"Okay," Emily said. "Now I need to borrow something old."

Rachel tugged a necklace from underneath her sweater, then unclasped it and handed it to Emily. "You can borrow this. It was Grandma Nettie's. I found it in the snow yesterday."

"You found it yesterday?" Rachel's dad asked. "Where?"

"It landed on my hand after the explosion. There was an earring tangled up in it."

"You're kidding." Emily examined the necklace, rubbing her fingers over the small diamonds. "This is beautiful. How do you know it's old?"

"If it was Nettie's, it's old," Virginia stated.

"Doesn't strike me as Grandma's taste." Emily held the necklace out for Justin to see. He pulled it closer and squinted, then gave her a smile and returned his attention to his phone.

Virginia took the necklace and examined it closely. "I thought I knew Nettie's whole collection, but I don't remember this necklace."

"Could have been a gift that didn't quite suit her." Dennis peered over his wife's shoulder. "Maybe she'd tucked it away somewhere."

"Why didn't you say something yesterday?" Cody asked. He had no idea what the necklace was worth, but he had to pay attention to any jewelry that might attract the attention of Richard Hammonds.

"I forgot about it."

When the necklace finally made its way back to Rachel, she refastened it around her neck.

"We'll have to go see if any other jewelry fell from the sky," Emily said with a laugh. "Justin, can you find time to go out to Nettie's and search? I'd love to wear the earrings too."

"I hope the firemen didn't step on or ruin anything," Virginia said. "Maybe Nettie hid other jewelry or money in the house."

"It's possible," Cody said. "People have been known to hide jewelry in air vents, behind loose bricks, or among cleaning supplies."

"I've heard of people putting their valuables in zipper bags and freezing them," Justin added.

The waitress came with their food, and everyone dug in while chatting about the wedding. Cody ate, but his mind wasn't on the meal. It was on all the different places a person might hide jewelry—and an elusive thief who would do whatever it took to get his hands on it.

Rachel was halfway through her meat loaf when Emily put her fork down and stared at their mother expectantly. "I'm ready when you are."

Her mom had spent lunch studying the color-coded to-do lists or scrolling through her phone. "Two more bites, then I'll be done."

Her father looked over at Rachel, his expression hopeful. "Are you feeling okay?"

"I'm fine. Not even a headache. I'm hoping Chief Becker will call, say the fire inspector has signed off, and tell me I can go through Grandma's house. Until then, I plan to head back to the lodge and rest."

"I'll be at the lodge too." Kristin pushed her plate away, her meal half-eaten. "If you need anything, Rachel, I'm there."

"Do you have any questions about your to-do list, Rachel?" Emily asked.

"No questions. I've already started writing the wedding toast, and I've scheduled an appointment to get my nails done."

Emily put her hand on Justin's arm. "Honey, what are you doing for the rest of the day?"

"I need to return some phone calls for work."

The waitress set the check in front of Rachel's dad. Justin reached over and snatched it. "I've got it."

"No, I'll get it," Cody protested.

Kristin stood up from the table. "Thanks for lunch. I need to get back. We're booked solid and I have some things to take care of."

"Miss Lambert?" Dennis asked.

"She's one of the things, yes."

Emily turned to Rachel and said, "I wish I hadn't scheduled your fitting today. It'd be fun to go shopping together, but I'm worried that would be too taxing for you now. We always had fun shopping in Aspen."

"We'll find some time," Rachel assured her.

Cody paid the tab, and everyone went about their day.

When Kristin offered Rachel a ride back to the lodge, Cody offered an alternative. "You can ride with me to Nettie's house and see what's going on with Becker rather than wait for his call. Maybe we can nose around to see if any other jewelry is hidden in the snow."

"I'd rather do that. But I need to make sure Timber's all right."

"I can check on him," Kristin offered.

"Okay, that would be great. If he's asleep, leave him be. If he's awake, will you take him out back? He'll know what to do. When you're ready to bring him inside, just say 'Come.'"

"He's that well-trained?" Kristin asked. "He'll obey a complete stranger?"

"As long as you use the commands he's used to and say them with authority."

Cody helped Rachel into his Jeep, and a few minutes later they were on the way to her grandma's.

"How elaborate was the bridal shower before Emily's first wedding?" he asked.

"A whole day event, starting with a trip to Telluride where we shopped for a good two hours before having lunch, followed by an afternoon at a spa and then back home for more food and for Emily to open her presents."

"You put that together?"

"No, Emily did with Kristin's help. It was a trying time for me."

"Because she was marrying Tyler?"

"Something like that."

"Do you want to talk about it?"

"No." The one person she'd ever talked to about it was Grandma Nettie, who had let Rachel cry on her shoulder and advised her granddaughter that, despite how hard it might be, only Rachel could decide whether she wanted to support Emily or pull away from the family.

In the end, Rachel had decided that if she wanted to stay civil with her sister after such heartbreak, she'd have to keep her distance.

"I've gone to two bachelor parties," Cody said. "At the first one, I was bored silly. The second, I'd been there all of twenty minutes before I got called in to work."

Rachel was glad he'd changed the subject. "I imagine that happens a lot."

"It really does." Cody rounded the corner onto her grandma's street. Rachel was relieved that there were no traffic jam or curiosity seekers. A cop car was parked in her grandma's driveway.

Cody took out his phone and called the police chief. "Becker, Rachel and I are outside. May we come in? Thanks." He climbed out of the car and came around to open her door before she even had her seat belt unbuckled.

"Is it a crime scene?" she asked.

"Not sure. The fire inspector signed off, so they want you to come in and see if anything is missing."

A minute later, she stood in the living room of her Grandma Nettie's cabin and felt an anger so deep it scared her. Somebody had trespassed in her grandmother's beloved home, and that hurt more than whether or not they'd caused the explosion.

"I'm glad you showed up when you did," Becker said to her. "I was about to call you. How are you feeling?"

"Better than yesterday. Have you found any sign of the man I caught fleeing after the explosion?"

"The deputy who was here yesterday found a few footprints by the back door, but with the snow, we couldn't really follow them."

"Of course," Rachel said.

"What I'd like you to do now," Becker said, taking a small notebook from his pocket, "is go from room to room and see if you notice anything missing or out of place."

"All right."

"We can start here in the living room. As you can see, you've got some water damage. Not as bad as it could be. Thanks to the snow, the fire department didn't need to douse everything."

Rachel forced a smile. "That's good, I guess." But it wasn't really. It was cold, and she worried the plastic draped over the gaping hole in the ceiling wouldn't be enough to keep out the elements, much less wild animals.

Other than that, the living room wasn't too bad. The floral couch had been pushed to the center of the room. The coffee table had been flipped on its side, the magazines stored under it scattered across the floor. Grandma Nettie's easy chair was by the door. The grandfather clock's hands stood still, and the dust on top suggested it hadn't been wound since Grandma Nettie's death. A painting on the wall closest to the hallway was cracked and had a broken frame.

The kitchen seemed all right. An old step stool stood by the back door next to an avocado-green gas stove. "That thing will outlive us all," Chief Becker commented.

A countertop took up one whole wall. The cabinets above it were glass, and Grandma Nettie's dishes were inside, miraculously unbroken. A clock was facedown on the floor, and a toaster sat in the sink with crumbs all around it. The refrigerator had come through unscathed, empty and unplugged as it was. The last wall had a small kitchen table for two, as well as the door leading to the living room.

Rachel went in and started opening drawers. All the silverware and pots and pans were where they belonged. The bread box held a few crumbs.

"Everything looks the way it should," Rachel said. "And, really, there was nothing here worth stealing."

"I keep thinking that if you had a squatter, they would have left a few dishes in the sink or some food on the counter." Becker put his notebook back in his pocket and asked Rachel, "Are you sure he was carrying a gun?"

"I'm sure." Rachel didn't like the doubt in Chief Becker's words. She moved into Grandma Nettie's bedroom, and Cody followed. The chair next to the bed still held one of her grandmother's sweaters, and a pair of slippers peeked out from under the bed. The dresser drawers were still empty. "Mom and Dad donated Grandma's clothes," Rachel explained. "Dad kept this sweater for sentimental reasons. It was her favorite."

"Makes sense," Cody said.

Framed photos covered the top of the dresser. Rachel righted a few that had fallen over. Grandma Nettie's jewelry box was there. Rachel opened a few of the drawers and fingered the colorful, bulky pieces.

"No one wanted the jewelry," she told Cody as Becker joined them.

"Same when my mother died," Chief Becker said.

"Show the chief the necklace you found in the snow," Cody urged.

"I didn't so much find it as it landed on me," Rachel reminded him, taking off the necklace and handing it to Becker. "During the explosion, when stuff was pelting me, this landed on my hand. There was a single earring too."

"Matching this necklace?" Cody asked.

"Yes, and if you compare this necklace to Grandma's other jewelry, you'll see they're not the same style."

"Maybe this was her most expensive set," Chief Becker said, returning the necklace, "and she only used it for special occasions. That's what my wife does."

Rachel shook her head, putting the necklace back on. "For really special occasions, my grandmother wore her squash-blossom necklace. She'd made it herself as a young woman in a silversmithing class. She used turquoise that had been mined by her father, and it took her a whole year to make. It's in our safe back home, along with Grandpa's watch. We didn't take any other pieces out of here."

"The set you found could have been a gift," Chief Becker pointed out.

"That's what my father said."

"Was there anyone who might have given it to her?" Becker asked.

"Maybe Bob Lewis, but it seems unlikely. He gave her an old mixer that didn't work. It was precious to him because it had been his mother's. Grandma Nettie kept it for a while because she didn't want to hurt his feelings."

"Yeah, Bob does like to give gifts," Chief Becker said. "He gave me the toy police car that sits on my desk at the station."

Rachel changed the subject back to the necklace. "My dad wondered if Grandma Nettie could have hidden this set of jewelry and the family didn't find it while we were cleaning."

"Stranger things have happened," Becker mused.

"Even stranger would be if some intruder saw this house and decided to start searching it for hidden treasure," Rachel said.

"It would have to be someone from out of town," Cody said. "Townies would know that Nettie didn't put much stock in material things. And, with the house next door up for sale, maybe somebody who came to an open house realized this one was empty and wanted a look inside."

"I doubt they'd have brought a gun though. The fact is, anything in here that's been disturbed—like the toaster in the sink—could be blamed on the explosion. I think once Chris Mack has a chance to assess the situation, we'll find that the water heater explosion was a fluke, and it was dumb luck that a hiker or trespasser happened to be nearby."

"With a gun?" Rachel asked.

"He wasn't aiming it at you, and there had just been an explosion. That might inspire me to draw my gun, even if I were on my way to see if anyone needed help. And I do carry a gun when I'm out hiking."

"But he saw Rachel," Cody said. "If he wasn't fleeing, why didn't he come back to help her?"

"I don't know, but that doesn't mean there's no logical explanation." Becker shrugged. "You mentioned finding a single earring too. I'd like to see it."

"It's on my bedroom dresser, back at the lodge." Rachel debated whether she should tell him why the earring had unsettled her. Finally she decided it was better for him to have too much information than too little. "You know," she said slowly, "my grandmother didn't have pierced ears, but the earring I found is for pierced ears."

"That's interesting," Becker said. "Can you bring it by the station later?"

"I'll go get it now." She and Cody headed out to his Jeep.

It was usually a twenty-minute drive to the lodge, but thanks to the slippery roads, it took almost half an hour. She could tell Cody wasn't happy with the delay.

"I'm glad Becker wants to see the earring," Rachel said.

"During an investigation, no rock is left unturned. He knew your grandmother. Maybe he'll recognize it."

"Nobody in the family recognized it."

"True," Cody agreed. He parked and hurried around to help Rachel from the Jeep.

They trudged through the parking lot, heads bent against the wind. When they reached the door, they hurried into the entryway and through the lobby, Rachel beginning to feel a new headache forming at the back of her neck. She waved at Kristin, who was busy at the front desk.

A minute later she stood in the middle of her room with Cody by her side, so close she could feel his warmth.

"This is really odd. Timber's sound asleep, and he always wakes when I enter a room." Rachel bent down, reaching into the crate to rub the top of Timber's head. Groggily, he peered up at her with his brown eyes before falling back to sleep.

"Timber, up." It was clear he didn't want to move, but he did, rolling to an upright position and coming out of the crate to lean against her.

"Is he all right?"

"Yes. But, if he's not more active by tonight, I'll call Dr. Levy."

With Timber at her side, Rachel walked to her dresser and then stopped. An embroidered doily and a family photo sat where they had been before.

The single earring, however, had vanished.

"The earring should be right here."

Cody was next to her in a second, picking up the doily and checking behind the photo. Nothing.

For the next half hour, they moved furniture. Cody crawled as far as he could under the bed, while Rachel felt along the edge of the carpet, opened dresser drawers, and emptied out the clothes.

But it was no use. The earring was gone.

7

"Are you sure you didn't misplace it?" Chief Becker asked.

"I put it right here," Rachel insisted, placing her palm atop the dresser. "And Cody and I searched every inch of this bedroom."

"They did," Kristin added from the doorway. "They came and got a flashlight from me."

"I helped move the bed," Justin said, peering over Kristin's shoulder. "And then I went and verified that housekeeping hadn't been in here."

"Was anything else out of place?" Becker asked Rachel.

"No."

"We can check local jewelers and pawn shops. Post an ad online," Chief Becker said.

"Do you remember exactly what it looked like?" Justin asked.

"It went with the necklace that fell on me after the explosion. I'm certain that the pieces were part of a set, though I have no idea where either earring is now." Rachel sighed. "I'm sorry, but I have another headache, and I'd like to lie down."

"Not much else we can do here," Becker said.

It was late afternoon when Cody returned to his parents' home, distracted. He should have stayed with Rachel a little longer to make sure she was all right. She'd been really spooked at the knowledge that someone had been in her room.

He didn't blame her. Nor did he believe for a minute that she'd misplaced it.

Heading to the basement, Cody sat and carefully laid the necklace across the top of his makeshift desk. After everyone had left Rachel's bedroom, he'd asked if he could borrow it to investigate and see if he could learn anything about it.

First, he took photos with his tablet and sent them off to head-quarters. Yes, it was a long shot, but the necklace was an exquisite piece that the family didn't recognize. Maybe it would match some of the jewelry that Hammonds had stolen.

He checked his emails, made a few notes on the Hammonds case, and then swept Rachel's necklace from the desk into a plastic bag, which he put in his coat pocket and zipped shut.

He pinned a note to the corkboard as part of his thinking wall. He was starting at the beginning, organizing Hammonds's crimes chronologically. His notes and photos fell into three categories: crime scenes involving no people, crime scenes involving police and victims, and potential sightings.

Two hours later, stiff from sitting still too long, Cody headed into town to Henderson's Jewelers.

The jewelry shop was located in an older section of town, with dusty red brick, a large picture window, and green awning sporting red and green flashing bells that chimed a continuous refrain of "Jingle Bells."

Cody pushed open the door and stepped in out of the cold.

"Cody? Hey, man!" Paul Henderson, dressed in a gray suit and white shirt complete with a tie, came around the counter. "Haven't seen you since high school."

Cody bumped fists with Paul. "What are you doing here? Last I heard, you were in Afghanistan."

"Around the time they closed the base, I had to decide whether to re-enlist or not. I chose not. I came home for a short visit, which became a long visit, and now I've taken over the store from my dad."

"Taken over?" Cody frowned. He didn't think Paul's father was old enough for retirement.

Paul's tone grew serious. "Dad decided that he wants to devote all his time to finding George." Kristin's missing fiancé was also Paul's brother. "I'm not going to lie—his obsession worries me. It's all he thinks about, and he's spending money right and left without any answers."

"It's hard when there's no closure," Cody said sympathetically. "There are entire organizations that focus on finding missing family members after law enforcement has exhausted their resources and time."

"Dad is in contact with one. I can't remember the name. He spends hours on their blog, reading stories and writing down the advice he gets."

"How long has George been missing now? Four years?"

"A little over."

"What does Kristin think of all this?"

Paul shrugged. "She says she's gotten on with her life and doesn't want Dad bringing it up. But the truth is, she won't leave Rolling Pine because she's afraid George will return and she won't be here. She's not even going to visit her parents for Christmas. She went for Thanksgiving, but only stayed two days."

"What about you? Do you think he might come back someday?"

"I don't know what to think. The military changed George, like it changed me. I served with quite a few men who cut ties and walked away from loving families."

Cody reflected on how torn his family would be if he or Todd simply disappeared. "I'll talk to your dad if I get the chance."

"I appreciate it."

"In the meantime, I've got a request for you." Cody pulled the necklace from his pocket. "Can you appraise a piece of jewelry for me?"

Paul went behind the counter, took out a velvety purple cloth, and spread it open. "Let's see what you have."

Cody arranged Rachel's necklace across the fabric. It was pretty against the purple material, he mused, but not as pretty as it had been on Rachel, where the sparkling gold had brought out flecks of amber in her brown eyes.

Paul whistled. "This is quite a piece. Do you want a ballpark estimate or a full report on the condition, quality and characteristics, style and technique, and so forth?"

"I need a detailed report if possible."

"Is this for insurance purposes?"

Cody hesitated, then produced his badge. "It's for a case I'm working on, so I need your discretion. You can't mention this to anyone, or that I'm a US Marshal. Not your wife, employees, or anyone else. And I'm sorry to ask, but do we need your dad's expertise, or are you qualified to provide the assessment?"

"I'm not GIA certified yet, but I can handle this. I've worked with my dad since I was a kid, going with him to purchase pieces at gem and mineral shows as well as making jewelry and selling it. I'll call my dad if you'd prefer, but I can do it if you want one less person in the loop on this."

Cody felt a little better. "Let's see what you find."

"If this is for a case, we don't want anyone walking in." Paul went to the front door of the shop, locked it, and flipped the door sign to *Closed*. He returned to the counter, moved a small light from a desk behind him to shine on the necklace, and took a microscope from beneath the display case.

Cody waited as Paul examined the piece.

"You have bezel-set stones here," he said.

"And that means?"

"There's a ring of metal enclosing the diamond. It's protective more than anything. My mother's favorite necklace is bezel-set, and it's from the 1700s."

"How old do you think this necklace is?"

"I'd say fifty years at most, making it vintage rather than antique. It's an Ankar necklace. The maker's mark is here on the clasp. They've been around since the seventies." Paul took a strand of diamonds from a drawer. Slowly, he held one of the Ankar diamonds against the different gems in the strand. "Your stones have no yellow. You definitely have a very expensive piece here." Paul fingered the necklace. "I see no flaws, and the cut of the diamonds is good. The accurate purity mark affirms the legitimacy of the gold."

"The what?"

"This 999 here," Paul said, pointing. "That means this is 99.9 percent gold, also known as twenty-four karat."

"Can you tell me how much you think it's worth?"

Paul took out a weighing scale. "If you want a precise estimate, I'll need to remove the diamonds from their mountings."

"I'd have to get permission from the owner for that."

"Okay, then all I can offer you is an educated guess." Paul worked the necklace and the scale, adjusting the position and squinting at the reading. "I'd say the stones' combined weight is about two and a quarter carats."

"Is that good?"

"Not good—spectacular. This necklace is probably worth about thirty thousand dollars."

Cody whistled. "What if it had matching earrings?"

"At the same quality as this? I'd say at least fifty thousand for the set. Easily."

"Impressive."

"You said it was for a case. Would you like me to go online and see if it's ever been reported stolen?"

"Yes please." Cody had already sent photos to the lab and planned to do that through his contacts, but the database that pawn shops and jewelry store owners used for tracking down stolen merchandise would tell him something immediately. He'd verify the findings with his own sources later.

"It hasn't been reported as stolen," Paul said a few minutes later. "Let me explore the diamonds' serial numbers and see what I find."

Before Paul could do so, someone knocked at the door. He swept up the necklace, wrapped it in a cloth, and locked it in the display counter. Then he let in Mrs. Banks, who gushed over an antique necklace Paul had restored for her, wrote a check, and patted Cody's cheek on the way out. "Your mama is so glad to have you home."

"Sorry," Paul said when the woman was gone. "You know Mrs. Banks. She'd have knocked until I let her in."

Thirty minutes later, Cody exited Henderson's Jewelers, necklace back in the plastic bag and tucked into his coat pocket. He also carried a borrowed metal detector with a waterproof coil. Paul had said it was perfect for finding jewelry in the snow but to expect to find a thousand bottle caps before locating the missing earring.

Cody was also fifty dollars poorer—he'd insisted on paying Paul for the appraisal—but richer in knowledge. Cody had a three-page report, both highlighting the condition of the diamond necklace in his coat pocket and documenting it as a commissioned piece. Five identical sets had been made—each with a necklace and pair of earrings—for a wealthy Nebraskan who had since passed on.

Cody intended to find out who'd received the sets. He seriously doubted Nettie Andrews had had any dealings with a millionaire who had lived in Nebraska. And if she had, she most certainly wouldn't have hidden such an expensive necklace from her heirs.

One thing was for sure. Rachel was going to be surprised when she realized she'd been walking around all day wearing a thirty-thousand-dollar necklace. He dreaded telling her the worth of the missing earrings.

And Cody was certain that whoever had taken the earring from her room knew exactly how valuable it was.

Rachel's headache was back in full force when she returned to her room after Cody and Chief Becker left. She checked on Timber, who was sleeping comfortably. She locked the door, wishing she had a dead bolt, took one of the pain pills her doctor had prescribed, and crawled under the covers. If someone hadn't violated her room and stolen her earring, she might have been able to nap peacefully. Instead, she tossed and turned.

Someone had been in her room.

She and Cody had gone over her belongings, and he'd surmised that whoever took the earring had only been searching for that one item, which Rachel had left in plain view.

Who would want her grandmother's earring, and a single earring at that?

Then there was the explosion.

Her last thought, before falling into a fitful doze, was to wish that Timber was back to his normal self. If he'd felt better, her dog would have barked and maybe the thief would have been caught.

Rachel woke when her phone pinged twice. She grabbed it from the nightstand and checked her messages. Her search and rescue partner back in Arizona had sent photos of some of the dogs going through their training. She responded to the message and then noted the time with a start as she realized she was running late for her meeting with Kristin, whose evening shift had ended twenty minutes ago. First, Rachel changed into less-rumpled clothes. Then she bent down to Timber's crate. He struggled to his feet before slowly following her outside.

Rachel dried him off and together they walked into the lobby, where Kristin was too busy to notice Rachel's tardiness as she dealt with an unhappy guest.

All Rachel caught from the overheard conversation was the word *stolen*.

"Can I help?" Rachel asked, joining them.

"I'm waiting for the lodge's owners to return. I'll share my complaints with them. I've already called the police." The woman glanced at Timber, pulled her sweater closer as if there were a chill, and glared at Kristin. "You have no security. None. This is ludicrous."

"Miss Lambert was in her room watching television when she realized she'd left her purse in her car," Kristin explained to Rachel.

"And immediately went down to retrieve it," added Miss Lambert. "It was gone."

"Where all did you go today?"

"That doesn't matter. I had it with me all day, going in and out of shops. The theft happened after I returned here. The thief has my identification, my credit cards."

"Did they break your car's window?" Rachel asked.

"They didn't need to. You touted how safe this lodge is, so I didn't lock my vehicle."

Justin came down the stairs, raised an eyebrow at the three women, and mouthed, "Do you need help?"

Rachel shook her head and returned her attention to the irate guest. "I'm so sorry this has happened to you, Miss Lambert. I'm sure a police officer will be here any minute."

"You have no idea how serious this is," Miss Lambert said.

"I assure you, my family doesn't take things like this lightly. I'll do everything I can to make this right. I'm Rachel Andrews."

The tall red-headed woman looked her up and down, one eyebrow raised. "Lydia Lambert."

"My parents own the lodge," Rachel said. "Let's check the lost-and-found bin while we wait for the police. Maybe someone found it and turned it in."

"I've been here all afternoon," Kristin said. "If someone handed in a purse, I'd know, and I'd have opened it to check for ID so I could return it. Miss Lambert, was your phone inside? If so, we might be able to use an app to find your purse."

"I have my phone," Miss Lambert said.

"Okay, let's check lost and found again, just in case."

The three women approached a locked closet, and Kristin unlocked and opened the door. She pointed. "Everything's labeled. The blue box is full of phone chargers. The yellow box has eyeglasses. Believe it or not, the three plastic bags to the side contain dentures. This red box contains keys. We no longer keep books or toiletries. However, we do get a lot of clothes, especially coats. When the weather gets warm suddenly, people forget they ever brought a coat."

Kristin pulled a plastic storage box from the floor.

In an instant, Rachel was pulled back to the explosion at her grandmother's, still in shock, seeing Timber hurt . . .

And watching as a man fled the scene, gun in hand, wearing a black coat exactly like the one on top of the pile right in front of her.

A police officer arrived at the lodge in response to Miss Lambert's call about her stolen purse. In addition to taking that report, the officer took possession of the black coat Rachel had noticed at the top of the lost-and-found pile, which was an exact match to the one worn by the man she'd seen leaving Grandma Nettie's house after the explosion.

The officer held up the coat. "They sell this brand over at Ludwig's Clothing. I've seen a dozen on the street today, if not more."

Great, Rachel thought.

Timber sniffed at the sleeves while the policeman held out the coat, clearly more interested in the outerwear than the officer was.

Before Rachel returned to her room, Miss Lambert urged them, "Leave no stone unturned."

The officer raised an eyebrow, bagged the coat, and left, promising to let them know if they found anything in either case.

Kristin leaned toward Rachel. "You did good. I think you even won Miss Lambert over. She's one of the most challenging guests we serve."

"She comes here often?"

"Yes, and she spends her days wandering the town. She's stayed here five times in the last four years."

"Does she come here to ski?" Rachel didn't think Miss Lambert looked the type.

"No, at least not that I know of. Your mom said Miss Lambert used to carry a picture she'd show around to people, asking if they recognized her cousin or some relative."

"Who was in the photo?"

"No one I recognized. Plus, I was fairly lost myself back then, what with George's disappearance."

Rachel reached over and squeezed Kristin's hand sympathetically.

The cell phone on the counter vibrated. Kristin picked it up and read the screen, then said, "Emily will be here in about thirty minutes. Let's get this shower finalized."

Rachel followed Kristin to an overstuffed brown sofa that faced a fire crackling in the hearth. She settled in its soft comfort with Timber at her feet.

"First, in all the excitement, I forgot to ask. How did things go at Nettie's?" Kristin asked. "Do they know whether the explosion was an accident or if the man you saw fleeing had something to do with it?"

"An accident, I think. Nothing's missing. There's no clear sign of an intruder inside and little doubt that the water heater blew. If it weren't for the fact that the man I saw in a black coat had no gear and was holding a gun, I'd have thought he was a winter hiker."

"It's a mystery," Kristin said.

Rachel nodded. "Let's put the finishing touches on this shower. I'm so glad Emily decided to keep it simple and have it at the coffee shop."

"This time it's honestly a low-key gathering. And I know you and Emily have had your challenges, but I think she does feel some remorse for what happened with Tyler." Kristin's voice softened. "I know that wedding must have been hard on you. I always wanted to tell you how sorry I was that you went through all of that."

"I know. Thank you."

"I know the way it happened wasn't right, but Emily truly loved Tyler. You weren't here much, and I understand why, but Emily hasn't been the same since he died."

"Until now?" Rachel asked.

"Not even now."

"I get the feeling you're not particularly excited about this wedding," Rachel said.

Kristin's brows knit and she frowned. "It's happening fast, and like I said, I'm not sure Emily has really finished grieving Tyler, if such a thing is possible. Losing someone you love—well, it crushes you," Kristin said. "It stays with you every day."

Rachel wasn't sure what to say. Emily losing Tyler was different from what had happened to Kristin. George was missing, presumed dead, so Kristin had no closure.

Rachel's phone rang, and she checked the screen. Even though she wanted to tell Cody about the black coat, she let his call go to voice mail. "Have there been any leads on George lately?" she asked Kristin.

"No, and it's a cold case now. Most of the town thinks he didn't want to be tied down and disappearing was the easiest thing."

"Is that what you think?"

"When he first went missing, I thought for certain that something had happened to him. Now I'm not so sure. His dad is still searching, though. If he has that much faith, how can I not?"

"The Hendersons are a close family," Rachel said.

"They also admit that George went through a tough time after high school. He got in so much trouble, but he changed after he went into the army. The George I fell in love with was caring, ambitious, and happy. He was in great shape with no medical issues and loved to hike whenever he could," Kristin said. "If he didn't just walk away, there should have been a body."

Rachel was at a loss for words.

They sat in front of the fire for a few minutes without speaking. Rachel hadn't known George Henderson well. He'd been two years ahead of Emily in school, meaning he'd graduated the year before

Rachel started as a freshman. She knew his younger brother, Paul, who had been one of her sister's friends.

"Okay." Kristin sat up straight, clutching the notebook. "Enough dwelling on the past. Let's get moving on this. Pining for Joe closes at two in the afternoon. They've agreed to reopen at seven and stay open until nine for the shower. We're ordering finger food, desserts, and coffee, and simply hanging out. Emily doesn't need any gifts, but I think she wants to have the shower to let Justin know that this second marriage is as special as her first."

"How many people will be there?" Rachel asked.

"About thirty. Your family and local friends."

"When is Justin's bachelor party? I didn't see it on my itinerary."

Kristin shook her head. "He's not having one. Personally, I don't think he has many friends. His brother's flying in to be his best man. Two of his college buddies and their families are on the guest list, but he seemed pleased when Emily said she wanted a small wedding."

When Emily married Tyler, there wasn't much about her future brother-in-law that Rachel didn't know, having dated him herself. Rachel knew little about Justin, and she and Emily weren't exactly close enough to talk about him. She would have to try not to let that bother her.

"So, what do you need me to do?" Rachel took the to-do list out of her purse, along with a pencil, and used the back of the paper for notes.

"You'll be in charge of a few games. Emily also wants cool prizes to go to the winners. Don't ask me what 'cool' means," Kristin said with a giggle. "I suggested gift cards and she wasn't a fan."

"I'll think of something." Folding her to-do list and assuring Kristin that she'd have everything ready for the shower, Rachel stood and made her way to the family quarters. Timber followed at her heels.

At the door, she turned to see Kristin staring at the flames as if lost in thought. Should she go back and assure Kristin that she'd find love again someday? No one could replace George, but it was possible to find someone who'd love, cherish, and build a life with her.

Deciding to leave things be, Rachel went to her room and filled Timber's food dish. He ate a little before nestling back into his crate. While he napped, Rachel settled at the desk to spend an hour catching up on her business back in Arizona. Then she sat cross-legged on the ground to rub Timber's head and ears before burying her face in the dog's fur. "Timber, up. Let's go," she said, pulling away.

It was clear the dog was reluctant, but he exited the crate. As he did, his back leg caught on the edge of the soft padding inside. It moved a bit, uncovering something sparkly.

Bending, Rachel gently pushed aside Timber's questing snout and rescued the shiny object—an earring, matching the one she'd discovered tangled up in her grandmother's necklace. It must have been tucked away in Timber's crate the whole time! Rachel reached for her neck, belatedly remembering that she'd given Cody the necklace for him to investigate.

Tucking the earring into her jeans pocket, she nudged Timber toward the door.

The Andrews home was quiet with the rest of the family still out. Rachel felt a tinge of concern. Roads were slick and the snow intermittent.

After slipping on her coat, boots, and gloves, she let herself out the back door and walked with Timber down a well-lit sidewalk. Timber didn't move with his usual pep. She'd intended to put him through some commands, but instead she brushed snow off a bench and settled down, enjoying the bracing night air as he flopped down in the snow beside her.

Something wasn't right.

She mulled over the events of the last two days—the explosion, being knocked unconscious, the earring's disappearance and reappearance, a guest's purse being stolen. She still didn't know what to think about the black coat. Was it just a popular brand and style favored by folks in the area, or did it belong to the suspicious man she'd seen at her grandmother's house?

Rachel eyed her usually active dog and made a decision. Pulling out her phone, she found Dr. Levy's number and started to make a call.

Timber growled and sprang to his feet. Rachel started to stand— when someone grabbed her from behind, pushed her down to the bench, and roughly placed a cloth across her face, covering her nose and mouth.

Chloroform.

She tried to hold her breath. She struggled, shoving at her attacker's arms.

No, no, no.

Cold fingers circled her neck and dug in while the other hand kept the cloth pressed against her mouth and nose.

She couldn't see, but she could hear. Why wasn't Timber barking or tearing into the man?

Rachel felt her consciousness slipping as the world around her became a murky haze until, finally, blackness settled over her like a blanket.

"Rachel!" Cody shouted. Her unmoving form sprawled on a bench. The sidewalk was slippery, but he didn't care. He ran to her side and pulled a towel from the lower half of her face. He moved her into a sitting position and rested his fingers against her wrist to take her pulse.

His mouth was dry as he waited for her to wake up. After way too long, her eyes fluttered open, and relief threatened to overwhelm him. But he needed to stay focused until he was certain she was going to be okay.

"Rachel?"

She didn't answer, but her breathing was even and her pulse felt strong underneath his fingertips.

"What happened?"

"I don't know. Timber and I were sitting here, and someone came up behind me and put that towel"—she pointed at the cloth he'd tossed aside—"over my face. I think I passed out."

"I think it's laced with chloroform. Someone meant for you to pass out."

Where was that person now? Had they disappeared into the woods? Into the lodge? Into a car from the parking lot?

Cody wanted desperately to go after them. But even more than that, he wanted to make sure Rachel was safe.

"Timber," she whispered, her voice groggy. "Where's Timber?"

"He's here on the ground. I think he's asleep." Pulling out his phone, Cody moved to make sure Timber was breathing. Then he called Chief Becker and Rachel's father.

He knelt in front of Rachel. "We'll take care of Timber. He's breathing fine, and I don't see any wounds. How are you feeling?"

Her eyes were huge with worry as she tried to stand and faltered. Cody helped her onto the bench and sat holding her until Dennis Andrews came running around the corner.

"We were just pulling in when Cody called," he said. "What happened, sweetheart?"

"Please take care of Timber while I get Rachel inside," Cody said, lifting her up in his arms.

Rachel's mother was at the door, holding it open and leading the way to the living room. Kristin was at her side with a blanket and a bottle of water in hand.

"Someone knocked her out on purpose," Cody said.

Virginia sat next to Rachel, putting a hand on her daughter's forehead. "What were you doing outside?"

"Timber probably needed to go out," her dad said as he entered the room, carrying the dog. Emily hurried over with a blanket and wrapped it around Timber.

"I'll call the vet," Justin said.

"Someone came up behind me," Rachel managed to say as her mother removed her heavy coat and boots to help her feel more comfortable.

"Did Timber give an alert?" Cody asked. "Do you remember anything else?"

Rachel winced, closed her eyes, and shrugged.

"I smelled chloroform," Cody told the family. "Meaning her mind is probably confused. It's amazing that she's even awake."

"Why would someone do that to her?" Kristin asked, sitting in the chair across from Rachel.

"I have no idea," Cody said, angry at the powerlessness he felt.

Justin came into the room, pocketing his phone. "I'm going to take Timber to Dr. Levy."

Emily fetched the crate from Rachel's room. As she and Justin were leaving with Timber, Chief Becker came in.

"Why don't you take Rachel to the clinic?" Becker suggested to Rachel's dad.

"Nothing they can do," Kristin said. "The chloroform is already wearing off. Her vision and hearing will be back to normal in a minute and you can start questioning her."

Becker and Cody stared at Kristin.

Kristin gave a slight shrug. "I watch every true crime show there is, and I listen to podcasts. She'll probably feel sick in a few minutes too, by the way."

Virginia was at Rachel's side in an instant to lead her from the living room into the bathroom.

Becker looked at Cody. "Did you find whatever the assailant used to cover her mouth?"

"It was a towel. I found it outside."

By the time Rachel and her mother returned, with Rachel clearly more alert, the two men were heading outside to search the area around the bench. Cody and Becker followed a set of footprints around the side of the lodge, but they were already disappearing under swiftly falling snow.

"My guess is he went into the forest," Becker said. "He wouldn't have gone into the lodge due to the cameras. Let's see what we can find out."

For the next hour, the police chief worked the case, questioning anyone at the lodge who might have seen anything or anyone unusual. Two deputies arrived and walked the surrounding woods. Cody helped as much as he could, circling back often to check on Rachel, who had mostly recovered.

When it became clear that the attacker was nowhere nearby, both Cody and Becker returned to the family quarters, where Rachel was sitting at the kitchen table drinking water, flanked by her parents and Kristin.

"Are you thinking what happened at my mother's house was intentional? That the explosion was set off to scare Rachel away?" Dennis asked, sounding deeply disturbed.

Becker shook his head. "I don't think so. All signs point to the water heater blowing up, and no one could have predicted what time Rachel would pull into the drive."

"Then this attack and the explosion are unrelated?" Rachel's father frowned. "What are the odds of that?"

"If it wasn't for the man Rachel saw leaving Nettie's house," Becker answered, "I'd say no odds. But that bit definitely throws a wrench into things."

"That man had a gun," Dennis said.

"We are certainly willing to investigate the possibility that someone was waiting for Rachel at Nettie's, and the water heater blowing was a fluke that might have saved her life, since it kept her from going inside. The black coat Rachel found earlier today has already been sent to the Denver forensic lab, where every hair or nail follicle attached to the material will be gone over." Changing focus, Becker asked Rachel, "Were you involved in a rescue lately that put you in harm's way?"

"No, nothing out of the ordinary. Plus, I'm never the lead."

"Think back as far as you can," Cody urged. "Does anybody have a reason to attack you?"

"No," she insisted.

It took another half hour before Becker left. Cody, Kristin, and Rachel's parents helped Rachel to her room. Emily and Justin found them there when they returned without Timber.

"Dr. Levy wants to keep him overnight," Emily said. "He said to tell you there's nothing to worry about. He just wants to do some precautionary blood work early in the morning. Are you sure you're feeling all right now?"

"I'm fine," Rachel said.

Her mother squeezed her arm. "Let us know if you need anything."

Virginia and Dennis went into the living room to watch the news while Justin and Emily headed to the kitchen.

"I don't like this," Cody said, sitting on the floor in Rachel's room while she took a seat at the desk.

"I'm not thrilled either."

"I tried calling you," Cody said. What he didn't say was that, had she returned his call, maybe he'd have been out there with her and the attack wouldn't have happened. But he quickly realized his agitation stemmed from the fact that he cared about her and had been worried. Thankfully, he'd been close enough to find her after she'd been knocked out.

"I'm sorry," Rachel said. "It's been an odd night. I'm sure Becker told you I found a black coat in the lost and found identical to the one I saw on the guy who fled Nettie's after the explosion."

"He did."

"Cody, there's something even stranger. I can't believe I didn't bring this up earlier, but everything is so fuzzy. The thing is, I was wrong before when I thought someone had stolen the single earring. No one broke into my room." Rachel stood, reached a hand into her jeans pocket, and pulled out the earring. "I found this in Timber's crate before I took him outside. I thought you and I had searched in there already, but it was tucked under the bedding. It must have fallen from the dresser and landed in the crate."

Cody took it, holding it under his phone's flashlight. "According to Paul Henderson, this could be a ten-thousand-dollar earring."

Rachel's jaw dropped. "You're kidding."

"Nope. I took your necklace into Henderson's Jewelers. Paul has taken over his father's store." Cody pulled the box from his pocket and handed it to her. "I had him appraise the necklace for a rough value."

"And?"

"The necklace alone is worth thirty thousand dollars. The stones are genuine diamonds, not cubic zirconia. And from what he said, they and the gold are both high quality."

"What?" Rachel stood, one stocking foot slipping on the hardwood floor. Cody steadied her until she sat again.

"May I borrow the earring to show to Paul? He says that if it's of the same quality as the necklace, it's worth around ten thousand dollars."

"Take it. Should I tell my parents the value?"

"Sure. But I wouldn't mention this to anyone else." He had a few more things he wanted to say but took note of her pale face and drooping eyes. "We can talk about this tomorrow. Right now, you need to get some sleep."

"I don't think—"

"Exactly," Cody said gently. "You can't think when you're this tired and have gone through this much. I think you should try to get some rest."

He helped her up and kissed her gently on the forehead before leaving the room.

Cody walked down the hall to join Rachel's mother and father in the living room. "Anything out of the ordinary—and I mean anything—please call me. I can be here in five minutes."

"Don't expect I'll get much sleep tonight," Dennis murmured, glancing meaningfully down the hallway toward Rachel's door.

Cody and the Andrewses said goodbye, and he left the lodge. He had a million things to do, none of which would get done if he did what he wanted, which was to sit in front of a roaring fire with Rachel tucked next to him so he knew she was safe.

Driving back to his parents' house, Cody reflected on the day. He arrived home and peered into the refrigerator, which his mother had packed with as many of his favorites as she could. Cody figured if he stayed in Rolling Pine more than a week, he'd have to go back to basic training to get rid of the weight he'd put on.

"If you don't want anything in there, I can get you something else," his mom said from the doorway.

"I'm just going to make popcorn, Mom."

"I'll make it for you."

He opened his mouth to stop her, but she was already fetching a microwavable packet from one of the cabinets. He busied himself grabbing a soda and some napkins. A minute later, he kissed his mother's cheek and headed down the stairs with his snack.

He took the earring from his pocket, put it in a plastic bag, and labeled it. Thanks to Paul's three-page report, he'd been able to profile the Nebraska multimillionaire who'd commissioned the necklace. Donald Allen had died back in 1975. He'd been married three times and had no children, but he did have a younger sister with five daughters.

Cody had pinned a photo of Allen to his corkboard. Strings secured with pushpins led to five nieces and their names and years of birth, all between 1920 and 1938. Four of Allen's nieces were deceased, and the last surviving niece was ninety-eight years old. Betty Manchester resided in an assisted-living residence and had two daughters, Tina and Monica, who both lived in Elkhorn, Nebraska.

Of the nieces who had passed away, three had died fairly young without offspring. The youngest niece, Rayna, had died ten years ago after a full life. It seemed Rayna had traveled to every continent and married well. Her obituary mentioned two daughters and three granddaughters. Rayna's remembrance website page showed her perched atop an elephant, her daughters Angela and Sheila behind her.

He needed to get to Elkhorn and pay a visit to the family. Quickly, Cody sent off an email to his superior, providing a brief description of the leads he was following and asking for all information available regarding Donald Allen's descendants.

Another issue Cody wanted to investigate was George Henderson's disappearance. He'd found the news report with the exact date George had been reported missing, four years prior. Next, he switched to the most easily accessible source of information available—social media.

Unsurprisingly, Kristin was on social media, but George's parents were not. Finally, fingers crossed, he looked to see if George had any social media accounts remaining and was pleased to find one.

Cody was tempted to start searching posts up to six months before George had gone missing. Instead, for the time being, he focused on the posts that had appeared on the anniversary of George's disappearance.

Kristin had written a post for George every July second.

Cody scrolled until he found the content from six months before George's disappearance. Then he got out a notebook, wrote George's name on the front in black marker, and then flipped the notebook open to the first page and drew a line down the center to form two columns. One he labeled *George*, the other *Kristin*.

Something Cody had learned as a law enforcement officer was that people loved to talk about themselves, and George Henderson had been no different. Prevalent were the posts about overcoming addiction. It appeared that George had gotten clean after a bomb killed two of his army buddies. Based on the photo of the destruction, George had been fortunate to walk away and change the direction of his life.

Cody wrote down the name of George's sponsor and the church that hosted his addiction program. Many of the posts showed George with his camera out in the forest, taking pictures of the landscape and the love of his life—Kristin.

There were three posts that really caught Cody's attention. The first was Kristin holding up her left hand, showing an engagement ring. The second was of the Grand Canyon and a pair of mules. Evidently George had booked a mule ride down to Phantom Ranch for a weeklong honeymoon adventure. The final post was of George and Kristin standing in front of a giant pine tree in the Arapahoe

National Forest, holding a handwritten sign that read, *This is the spot where we're getting married next week.*

In Cody's experience, those who disappeared were usually fleeing a life they could neither bear nor control, which did not at all match George's situation. George and Kristin had seemed happy as they looked forward to a future together.

Cody closed his notebook, switched out the light, and headed upstairs to a bedroom still decorated with track awards, an outdated Wi-Fi speaker, and a stack of PC games that modern high schoolers would laugh at.

The nightstand had an alarm clock he would never use again because his phone was a better option. Next to it was the Bible his grandpa had given him when he was twelve. Grandpa had been Rolling Pine's chief of police long before the current chief, Becker, was old enough to say, "Stick 'em up."

Cody settled into bed. Right before dozing off, he admitted to himself that he wished he'd stayed on the couch in the Andrewses' living room to keep Rachel safe.

9

*R*achel's eyes flew open. For a moment, she wanted to close them. Maybe then she could forget last evening, the feeling of fingers around her throat, and the fear of knowing someone wanted to cause her physical harm.

And her room was too quiet. She was used to Timber's odd sleeping noises. They'd been a team for so long that she felt a bit lost without him.

It was harder than usual to step out of bed, get dressed, and face the mirror, where she noticed the fingertip-size bruises across her neck.

Rachel needed to be with people.

"How are you feeling?" Emily came into the bathroom and stood barefoot beside Rachel, feeling for all the world as if they were both back in high school.

"Confused," Rachel admitted.

"But not in pain?" Emily brushed the hair away from Rachel's neck and studied the bruising. She sucked air through her teeth in sympathy.

"No, no pain. It could have been so much worse."

"And you have no idea who attacked you or what they wanted?"

"None."

"We can cancel the wedding shower," Emily said softly. "It's not a big deal."

Rachel was touched. That evening was supposed to be her sister's night to shine, and so far Rachel had been in the limelight since she'd arrived—though not by choice.

The sisters left the bathroom. "It'll be fine. Your shower is in bold on my list," Rachel said as the sisters strolled into the kitchen.

"Mine too." Kristin walked straight to the fridge, where she grabbed eggs and bacon. "And in capital letters. 'Emily's shower Tuesday evening.' I think there are at least five exclamation points too. As if I could forget." She winked.

"Did you find everything you needed in Aspen yesterday?" Rachel asked Emily.

"We must have gone to seven different stores, but I finally found the perfect cake topper. It's much better than the one I ordered online."

"Hi, honey." Justin walked in, gave Emily a peck on the cheek, and poured himself a glass of milk.

"You're up early," Emily said.

"I told your dad I'd go with him and Rachel to search for the other earring."

"You're the best." Emily flung her arms around him.

Rachel and Kristin playfully rolled their eyes at each other.

Turning to Rachel, Emily asked, "Are you sure you're up to it?"

"I'm as surprised as you are, but I really feel fine." She'd started feeling better the night before.

A few minutes later, Rachel's parents joined them.

Rachel pulled her plate close and dug in, before casually mentioning, "Cody took the necklace to Henderson's yesterday to get it appraised."

"Good idea," her dad said. "What did he find out?"

Rachel reached up and unclasped the necklace, laying it on the table in front of her plate. "Apparently it's worth thirty thousand dollars."

"W-what?" her mother stammered.

"We need to put that in the safe." Her father picked up the necklace. "I had no idea Mom had anything this valuable. I wonder why she didn't put it in her safe-deposit box."

Rachel held up a hand. "The necklace and the earrings are a set. Granted we just have the one and the other is still missing, but—"

"But even alone, the earring is worth a great deal," Emily added.

"How do you know that?" Justin asked.

"Cody says it's part of a set that was commissioned over fifty years ago, made by a designer named Ankar," Rachel explained. "Paul was able to look it up."

"Commissioned by whom?" her dad wanted to know.

"A wealthy man named Donald Allen, from Elkhorn, Nebraska. He had five sets made for his nieces."

"Never heard of him," her dad said.

"There's no one with the last name of Allen on the family tree," Virginia added.

Rachel believed her. Virginia Andrews took pride in her husband's family name and the fact that an Andrews had been one of the first settlers in the area and had helped name Rolling Pine. Rachel's family still owned several downtown properties, as well as a few rental houses and the lodge.

"So," her mom asked the pivotal question, "how did Nettie come by the necklace?"

"It's a mystery," Rachel said.

"Which finding that second earring will help solve," Emily said pointedly.

Justin shrugged good-naturedly. "Let's do it."

Kristin finished the last of her breakfast, stood, and said, "Why don't you let me put the necklace and earring in the safe behind the front desk?"

Dennis handed over the necklace, but Rachel said, "I gave the single earring to Cody after I found it in Timber's crate. He wanted to take it to Paul to make sure it matches the necklace."

"What are the odds that we'd find such an awesome necklace and earrings in time for me to wear them at my wedding?" Emily asked, eyes sparkling.

Justin stood and took his plate to the sink. "If we're going to search for jewelry, I can only spare a few hours this morning. I need—" His phone pinged before he finished. Glancing at the screen, he said, "Good, my brother. He was going to try to get an earlier flight." He stepped out of the kitchen to take the call.

Emily lowered her voice and addressed Rachel. "Jerome is all the family Justin has left. His parents and younger brother were killed in a car crash a decade ago."

"So sad," Virginia murmured.

"He loves our family," Emily went on, "and the sense of community here. I guess they traveled a lot, so there wasn't much of a permanent home. He's amazed that we know everyone in Rolling Pine."

"Working for me, he'll soon know everyone and their secrets," Virginia said.

Justin came back into the room, his features drawn tight.

"What's wrong?" Emily asked.

"It's Jerome. He can't come. Apparently he's been called to testify in court on Friday for a work thing. Some breach of contract."

"That's not a good enough reason," Emily protested.

"The company's being sued for over six million dollars. He'll lose his job and possibly be arrested if he doesn't appear in court."

"Why is he finding this out now?"

"It was unexpected. I guess his name came up during an interview. You have no idea how sorry I am."

Emily straightened, "We'll have to find someone to take his place. The tux is rented. How about one of your high school friends?"

"Why can't Paul stand up with me by himself?"

"Because I have two attendants."

"I don't mind walking down the aisle unescorted," Kristin said. "Or, actually, I don't mind just being a guest."

Emily pinned Kristin with a fierce glare. "No chance."

"I'll call one of my college buddies and make it happen." Justin bent to kiss Emily on the cheek. "I'm heading out to the garage to find some extra shovels and a rake."

"I haven't shoveled in years," Dennis said. "First time I'm actually excited about it. Honey, you coming to help?"

Her mom shook her head. "I'm showing a house in an hour. I need to get to the office."

"Mom," Emily scolded, "you said you were taking this week off. I was hoping you'd help me with the last of the table toppers."

"I know, sweetie, but the client couldn't meet any other day. You and Kristin will do fine. Get Rachel to help."

It all sounded so normal. Emily, of course, was the center of attention. Levelheaded Kristin was getting things done. Their mother was present, but thinking about work. Dad went with the flow. He was where he wanted to be, running the lodge. Justin seemed to fit in well, but he wasn't anything like Tyler. Rachel wondered what Tyler would have made of the necklace and earring. He'd probably agree with her that they signified more mystery than treasure, and she worried they came with a price the Andrewses might not want to pay.

Cody hadn't gotten much sleep. The heater had kicked on and off all night, keeping him awake. But maybe it wasn't the noise. Maybe it was his mind being on high alert, grappling for ideas that could lead him to Richard Hammonds. He finally stopped pretending once the sun came up. His father had returned home late last night, so Cody knew to be quiet as he slipped into jeans and a T-shirt. He carried his boots and tablet down to the kitchen.

He poured a bowl of cereal and settled at the kitchen table, where he could see Nettie's house through the window. Except for the blue plastic tarp still covering the gaping hole near the water heater, it looked as it had for his entire life. Nettie's backyard melded with the Arapahoe National Forest, where long ago he, the Andrews girls, and their friends had built tree houses, forts, and an army of snowmen.

He finished his first bowl and started on a second before taking out his tablet and opening his email. A report from his superior verified what Cody already knew. The necklace didn't match any of the jewels taken during Richard Hammonds's known heists. Nor did it match any reported missing jewels.

Cody probably didn't need to waste time checking out the earring, but something about the value of the jewelry, the Andrewses' surprise at its existence, as well as the story of the five women who'd received the sets compelled him.

That, and Rachel's company.

Cody stood, leaning forward to get a better view out the window, glad it had stopped snowing, and noticed someone near Nettie's house. Male. Wearing a dark coat, walking around in the snow. Cody immediately stepped into his boots, slid his gun into his waistband, and was on his way out the door when he noticed another figure join the first one.

Rachel.

Cody's heart skipped.

Rachel pointed at something, and the black-coated figure headed in that direction. Okay, so not every man who wore a black coat near Nettie's house was a bad guy. There had to be a million black coats.

But there's only one Rachel.

His heart returned to normal when he noticed Timber limping at her side. Poor guy. Cody had been worried about Rachel's dog.

Cody headed back inside, rinsed his bowl, set it in the sink, and grabbed his coat and gloves on the way out.

The metal detector Paul had lent him was in the back of his Jeep. He grabbed it and jogged over to Nettie's. "You're out here early," he called.

Dennis stood on the front porch, cheeks red from the cold. "When Rachel shared how much the necklace and earrings are worth, we got excited."

"Emily wants to wear the earrings and necklace for the wedding," Justin said, coming to stand by Dennis. "She added searching for it to my list."

"Is Emily here with you?" Cody asked.

Rachel came around the corner, brushing her gloves against each other to dislodge a bit of snow. "No, Emily has a million things to do, and she's confident that we'll find it."

"Good to see Timber," Cody remarked.

"They think he might have been drugged, but not with chloroform like me."

Which meant that the attack on Rachel had been planned. Before Cody could think of what to do or say next besides getting the lump out of his throat, Justin joined them, holding up a metal detector and asking, "Where did you get yours?"

"Paul Henderson loaned it to me. You?"

"Justin found it in the garage," Dennis answered. "We're pretty sure a guest left it at the lodge years ago. Sure surprised us that it actually works."

"Did you all find anything before I got here?" Cody asked.

"Pennies, nails, bottle caps, pieces from the water heater, and an old ring," Rachel said proudly. "Unfortunately, it has no relation to the necklace and earring. Want to see?"

"Of course."

Ordering Timber to stay outside, Rachel led the way inside to the kitchen, where the ring lay on a blue washcloth. "I tried to clean it with soap and water, but that didn't help much."

Dennis picked it up, almost caressing it. "It could have been out there since before the house was built."

Gazing at the ring, Cody was suddenly very aware that he'd spent time investigating a necklace that probably really did belong to Nettie and had nothing to do with Richard Hammonds. He'd also spent time researching the disappearance of George Henderson, which had nothing to do with the Richard Hammonds case. And now he was musing over an old ring, probably lost before Richard Hammonds was even born.

Later that day, he needed to focus on the case and document something other than Grandma Nettie's jewelry.

But he also knew that, had the thief been in the area, Richard Hammonds would certainly be interested in the Ankar necklace and earrings. Cody had a hard time believing the explosion, the previous night's attack on Rachel, the jewelry, and the fleeing man were all coincidence. There had to be a connection. And, while "gut feeling" wasn't enough before a court of law, that very sensation had been the starting point of many a solved case.

"You need to be careful not to publicize the monetary value of the necklace and earring," he reminded Rachel, making sure both Dennis and Justin heard.

"No one except the family and you know the value," Rachel said.

And Kristin and Paul, Cody mentally added.

Justin checked his watch. "At most, I can put in another hour searching. I can't blow off the rest of my to-do list. I have to be alive in order to get married, and Emily will kill me if I don't pay the DJ and florist. Plus, apparently, I need to find a new best man and write a speech."

"I have to write a speech too," Rachel said.

"Why do you have to find a new best man?" Cody asked.

"Something came up with my brother's work. Hey"—Justin sized Cody up—"You could stand up for me. What size suit do you wear?"

Cody took a step back. Was it possible that Justin didn't know his history with Emily? It was one thing to attend Emily's wedding, but it was quite another to be in it. "No thanks. I'm not the best-man type."

"Please?" Justin pressed. "The wedding's in four days. I only have Paul to stand up with me."

"Paul Henderson?" Cody asked.

"Yeah, Paul's a solid guy. We met at the gym. He's a good racquetball player."

Dennis leaned on his shovel and studied Cody. "It would mean a lot to Emily."

"My college roommates are coming up," Justin said. "I was going to ask one of them, but one is six inches shorter than my brother, and the other is a hundred pounds heavier. The tux wouldn't fit either of them. You, however, are roughly the same size as Jerome."

Rachel moved to stand next to him, putting her hand on his arm and saying low enough that no one else would hear, "It would mean so much to my sister. I'll be standing up for her."

How could he say no? Hoping his forced smile didn't show how much he truly did not want to agree, he asked, "Where do I get the suit?"

"I'll let Emily know. She'll text you the information." Justin slapped Cody on the back and picked up his metal detector before heading for the front of the house.

Dennis grinned and followed.

"You get the idea they know something we don't?" Cody asked.

"They know it's best to keep Emily happy," Rachel responded.

The four of them got to work, uncovering five empty soda cans, three pennies, nine nails, and a dozen broken metal odds and ends. After an hour, Dennis and Justin left.

About the time Cody's back started protesting and his fingers froze, Rachel let out a shout. "I found something!"

Cody got to her side and helped her to her feet. "What is it?"

"A bracelet," she said, holding it out for him to see.

There'd been no mention of a bracelet by Paul or in the US Marshal's report from that morning. If the shimmering diamonds in her hand were of the same quality as those in the necklace, he figured the Andrews family owned almost a hundred thousand dollars in Ankar jewels.

Cody had expected to find an earring, which would have brought a sort of closure. The discovery of a bracelet, however, changed everything.

As his stomach filled with dread, Cody ruminated that the more jewelry Rachel found around her grandmother's home, the more danger lay ahead.

$\mathcal{T}$he bracelet, zipped tightly in Rachel's coat pocket, was as light and delicate as the necklace and earrings. Yet, in her mind, it weighed a ton—a five-digit ton. She followed Cody across the street and down to his vehicle, opened the back door, and helped Timber into the back, where he shook snow, ice, and water across the seats.

She winced. "Sorry."

He grinned. "No problem. Dogs will be dogs."

Settling into the passenger side—something that was becoming a pleasant habit—Rachel said, "With all this mysterious jewelry, I'm starting to think Grandma must have had some kind of secret life or a secret boyfriend."

Cody laughed and fired up the Jeep so it would warm up. "I'm going to run into my parents' house and get the earring before we go visit Paul. I'll be right back."

Rachel used the time to check on Timber. He sat bolt upright on the passenger-side back seat, all happy wet-dog-smell canine. Planning ahead, she pulled her phone from the zipped pocket and verified with the veterinary clinic that she'd be stopping by again that afternoon.

Cody finally burst out of the front door, looking like a man of action. She'd always loved that about him. Actually, her heart corrected softly, she had always loved *him*. He'd been such a good friend when they were younger. Was that how he still saw her? Or did he see her merely as his ex-girlfriend's little sister?

If she were honest, she'd have to admit that neither of those was enough—not really. She wanted more than friendship.

"I called Paul and told him about the bracelet and the information I found out about Donald Allen," he said, sliding behind the wheel and closing the driver's side door. "He's expecting us."

"What do you think he'll tell us that we don't already know? I think we can estimate the worth of the bracelet. And, if you want to keep this a secret, should we involve Paul?"

"The bracelet's a surprise. According to both Paul's and my research, there's no record of it. So maybe it's not an Ankar. Before I dig deeper, I need to know as much about it as he can tell us. And he already gave an appraisal on the necklace, so he's aware of the situation."

Rachel wasn't entirely convinced, but she trusted Cody. "I've been trying to come up with an idea of who might have given Nettie the jewels and I can't think of anyone. After Grandpa died, the only man I ever saw her in company with was Bob Lewis, but he was just a friend. They sometimes played rummy on her front porch."

"Bob is definitely harmless, but he is known for giving out gifts."

"Strange gifts."

He reached across the seat divider and gently touched Rachel's upper arm. If they'd not been covered in snow gear, it might have been romantic. She felt much the way she had in high school when she'd suddenly realized Cody was standing close to her. His presence had always felt different, more special, than anyone else's. And she had taught herself to ignore, or perhaps disguise, her feelings for him.

He pulled his hand away and set it on the steering wheel. Cody wasn't a teenager anymore. He was a grown man, and her attraction to him had simply increased in their time together over the past couple of days.

"I'll figure this out," he said. "And I won't let anything else happen to you."

She blinked, surprised by a sudden rush of emotion.

"You all right?" he asked.

"I'm worried about Timber. After we leave Paul's, do you mind if we run by the veterinary clinic?"

"Not at all."

"Good," she said, "because I already made the appointment."

He chuckled. "Of course you did."

She glanced at the back seat where Timber slumbered peacefully. "I can help you clean up the back there. He's gotten the floorboards and seats dirty."

"It's nothing," Cody said. "I'm glad to have you both with me."

They hit Main Street and snagged a parking place in front of Henderson's Jewelers. After checking that Timber was still sleeping, Rachel exited the car as Cody came around to help her.

Inside, Christmas decorations were minimal but sale items plentiful. Paul was already helping one customer, with a second waiting in line, so Rachel started exploring. Signage told her she could purchase one pair of earrings and get the second pair for half price. If she purchased a watch today, she qualified for free cleanings for the next ten years. Had she ever kept a watch that long? Did she want to?

Cody took off his coat and settled into a seat by the back wall. He immediately took out his tablet. Moments later, whatever he was reading had him mesmerized.

Rachel took off her gloves, stuck them in her coat pocket, and continued to browse. Finally the other customers left with their purchases. Paul stepped from behind the case, flipped the sign to *Closed*, and locked the front door.

"Why are you locking it?" Rachel asked.

"So we won't be disturbed."

Cody said, "I've told her the approximate value you estimated, and that the family is keeping this under wraps."

"I can't imagine this bracelet would be part of the set," Paul said, resuming his place behind the counter. "The five sets commissioned by Donald Allen for his nieces only consisted of a necklace and a pair of earrings each."

Rachel unzipped the inner pocket of her coat and pulled out the bracelet. She watched as Paul draped it over a purple cloth. Next, Cody handed over the single earring. Paul frowned and put them next to each other.

"What?" Cody asked.

"Give me a minute." Paul retrieved a jeweler's loupe and picked up the bracelet. He moved it back and forth under a small lamp, examining the stones, then studied the earring.

Rachel pulled out her phone and took advantage of the bright light to snap photos of the jewelry.

Finally Paul said, "The bracelet is Ankar, like the necklace, just shy of three carats. It must have been made at a later date. I estimate its worth at slightly more than the necklace. I wonder if there are also five bracelets."

"So, is it a set?" Cody asked. "Necklace, bracelet, earrings? Provided we find the missing earring."

"No," Paul said confidently.

Picking up the earring, the jeweler ran a finger over the single stone. "This is not Ankar, and these stones are cubic zirconia, not diamonds. It's a mass-produced earring that you can buy at any tourist store in town for under twenty dollars."

"But the earring was tangled up in the necklace," Rachel said.

"Paul, can you bring up a picture of the Ankar earrings that would go with the bracelet and necklace?"

A minute later all three of them gaped at the computer screen.

"It's the same length as the one I found," Rachel said. "And I thought it was gold, with three rows of gems."

Paul held up the earring. "So this is definitely the one you found?"

Rachel squinted at it. "I'm not sure. It looks a little thinner."

"But you're not certain," Cody said.

"I barely glanced at it," Rachel said. "I didn't have a chance to analyze it."

"You knew you'd placed the earring on your dresser," Cody said.

"One hundred percent."

"And we searched your room together."

The front bell sounded, and Chief Becker peered in through the window.

"Probably a good thing he's here," Cody said, walking over to unlock the door.

Becker stamped snow off his boots and said, "I don't know what it is, Rachel, but since you've returned to town, there's been nothing but excitement."

"It's not my fault a house exploded."

"Are you doing okay?" the chief asked.

"Much better. Timber's sleeping in Cody's Jeep. He's fine too, but we're taking him to the vet later to be safe."

Cody said, "Adding to the excitement, there's something you need to know. Paul, why don't you tell him about the jewelry?"

Paul shared their findings, showing the chief the Ankar set on his computer screen.

Cody chimed in when the jeweler was finished. "I believe someone was in Rachel's room twice. First to steal the Ankar earring off her dresser, and later to replace it with a fake, which Rachel found in Timber's crate. They might have drugged her dog the second time, to keep him quiet."

Rachel gasped in horror. "They went after my dog?"

Cody took her hand. "I don't know that for sure, but I do know that we're going to get this guy. I promise."

Becker listened intently. "You're just now telling me this?"

"Things have been moving quickly. I realized it about thirty seconds before you got here." Cody tightened his jaw before asking, "Can I speak freely?"

Becker raised an eyebrow at him. "You can, but are you sure you want to tell?"

"Civilians are on a need-to-know basis," Cody said. "Right now, Paul and Rachel have information that could put them in harm's way. In Rachel's case, it already has. I think it's time."

Rachel stared between them. "Time for what?"

"I'm a US Marshal, and I'm in town working on a case," Cody explained. "Emily's wedding couldn't have come at a better time. It enables me to investigate under the radar. Except, thanks to Rachel, I'm not under the radar any longer."

Rachel frowned. "Like I said, it's not my fault Grandma Nettie's house exploded."

Cody went on. "A whole lot of things that shouldn't be related are suddenly coming together. I can try to rationalize that there's a good chance your grandmother received the necklace and bracelet as some sort of gift—perhaps from Bob Lewis—and hid them away, but I can't rationalize how the man in the black coat with a gun is involved."

"Or why I was attacked last night," Rachel said.

Cody looked at her, green eyes intense. "I'm sure he's after the jewelry. Last night, I'll bet he thought you'd be wearing the necklace."

Rachel put a hand to her throat. "That's why his hands were around my neck."

"Exactly." Cody leaned toward her. "So, Rachel, I need you to understand that whoever this guy is, he's watching you. You found the necklace, the earring, and the bracelet. Until we catch him, you're stuck with me. I'll be your bodyguard from now on."

"But—"

"But nothing," Cody interrupted. "Someone's been in your room. Twice. And you've been attacked. Which is why I'd like to ask Paul to lock the bracelet in his safe, for now."

"I can do that," Paul agreed.

Rachel ran a fingertip over the substitute earring, still displayed on the purple cloth. "One tiny thing, one big problem."

Rachel sat quietly as they drove to the veterinary clinic. She briefly considered heading for Aspen and buying a plane ticket back to Arizona.

But her family was in Rolling Pine. And if she left, whoever was after her might go after her family. She couldn't allow that.

Cody pulled into Dr. Levy's parking lot. "Head on in. I'm going to call your dad with an update. He needs to be alert and careful."

Rachel hopped out, attached Timber's leash, and headed for the porch, barely registering Dr. Levy's festive Christmas decorations as she entered a crowded waiting room and found Bob Lewis waiting with his dog.

"I think Biggles is getting arthritis in his hips," Bob confided to Rachel after she checked in and sat down. "He and I are alike that way."

Rachel nodded, distracted by a box full of golden retriever mix puppies at Elmore Banks's feet.

"Someone left them at the end of my driveway," Mr. Banks told Rachel as Cody entered and sat next to her. "Probably knew my wife is a soft touch. They weren't but a couple of weeks old at the time. I've done nothing but bottle-feed the little things since then, which is not how I expected to spend retirement. Nine altogether. Want one?"

Cody shook his head. "Not right now."

The woman sitting next to Mr. Banks leaned forward. "You're Rose's son, Cody. I don't know if you remember me. I'm Kate Welch. You came into the coffee shop yesterday morning."

"I remember. You make awesome brownies."

"Thanks. This is going to be the best Christmas ever. I came in here to ask Doc Levy if he knew of any dogs that needed a home, and Mr. Banks was here with these beauties. It's fate." She reached into the box and pulled out a wriggling blond puppy. "My husband wanted a two- to three-year-old rescue, housebroken, midsize. Boy, will he be surprised when I come home with a puppy. Think he'd mind if I brought home two?"

Rachel laughed and moved over to sit next to Kate. She motioned for Timber to sit, then stroked the puppy's head. "I'm Rachel Andrews. My sister, Emily, is having a bridal shower at your coffee shop tonight."

"I'm so glad to run into you. We closed at two, and for the last two hours we've done nothing but decorate."

"Decorate? Was I supposed to help with that?" Quickly, Rachel pulled her to-do list from her purse. "No, decorating is not listed, but organizing three games and having prizes is."

"Is that a party-planning list?" Kate peered over Rachel's shoulder. "What kind of games are you doing?"

Rachel flinched. "I'm not sure yet."

"We've been busy," Cody put in.

"Oh, yeah, I hear you've been searching for the stuff that blew out of your grandmother's cabin when it exploded. And that you were attacked last night. I'm so sorry about that. Are you all right?"

"Right as rain." Rachel smiled, amazed as always by how fast news traveled in Rolling Pine.

"I tell you what," Kate said. "Let me put together the games and prizes."

Rachel didn't hesitate. "That would be great. Make sure to save your receipts so I can reimburse you."

"Perfect." Kate leaned over and rubbed the top of Timber's head. "Man, your dog is so well-behaved. I've never seen anything like it."

"Timber is a search and rescue dog."

"That's remarkable," Kate said. "Years ago, when I lived in Montana, my little brother got lost in the woods behind our house. I still remember all the dogs and handlers that came to comb the area."

Rachel put her hand on Kate's arm. "They found him?"

"Mikey was six," Kate said, her voice soft. "He was lost for two days, but they found him—tired, hungry, and scared."

Emotion welled in Rachel's heart at the story's happy ending. She stroked the puppy in Kate's lap. "He might make a good search and rescue dog. Goldens are super intelligent and trainable, and have the fortitude and stamina required."

"The one you picked out already has a good sniffer," Mr. Banks chimed in. "My wife keeps hiding her favorite slippers, and this one keeps finding them."

"I wouldn't know how to train him," Kate said. "I've never had a dog."

"It's a huge investment of time. I've probably put eight hundred hours into working with Timber." Hearing his name, Timber looked at Rachel inquisitively. When she didn't give him a task, he lay down, putting his head on his legs, tongue lolling happily.

"Wow." Kate shook her head. "With our new business, I'm lucky if I have *eight* spare hours a week. But if we adopt this little guy, I'm going to carve out more time and hire a dog sitter when I can't be home."

"Dog day camps are also a great option," Rachel said. "They give your dog a chance to socialize with other dogs as well as humans."

"I'm coming to the shower," Bob said, joining the conversation. "I have a very special gift for Justin. We have breakfast together sometimes. And I have an even more special present for Emily. She'll love it."

"I'm sure she will," Rachel agreed.

Before Bob could say anything else, the door separating the foyer from the examination rooms opened and the receptionist beckoned to him. He got up and disappeared down the hallway with Biggles.

Kate excused herself. "I've got some games to plan and gifts to retrieve."

Cody watched her go, then said to Rachel, "You do know that all the prizes are going to be Pining for Joe gift cards, coffee mugs, and coffee-themed T-shirts."

"Yes, that's occurred to me. Shower gifts of T-shirts that say 'All of Rolling Pine is Rolling into Joe's for Coffee' might not be what Emily meant by 'cool.' I really wanted to make amends."

"If you want to share what happened between you and Emily, I'm a good listener. Believe me, I have a career that includes hearing confessions."

Rachel issued a small laugh. "No, but thanks for the offer."

Bob came back through the door, and Cody stood. "Bob, got time for a few questions?"

At that moment, Mr. Banks came out of the second examination room and asked, "Cody, can you carry the puppies back to the car for me?"

"Wait for me," Cody told Bob.

Cody took the box of puppies from Mr. Banks, who opened the door and let in a burst of cold. They both headed into the snow. Bob followed, but Rachel noted that he turned left instead of following Cody to the right.

By the time she shimmied back into her coat and made it to the door, Bob had disappeared and Cody was watching as a neat luxury sedan pulled into the parking lot, out of place next to all the SUVs and trucks and Dr. Levy's work van.

"Hi, Cody," Justin said as he got out of the car. "Why are you out here in the cold?"

"Did you see which way Bob Lewis went?"

"I sure didn't."

Justin walked with Cody back to the clinic. After they came inside, Justin said to Rachel, "I've been looking all over town for you. Emily's going crazy. Are you all right? Have you checked your phone lately?"

Rachel took her phone from her coat pocket. "Oops, I had the sound off. Thirteen calls, all from Emily."

"Something wrong?" Cody asked.

"She has a million things to do and her stress level's going through the roof," Justin said. "Any chance you'll be home soon?"

"Right after Timber sees the doctor. He should be next."

"I can wait and take you. That will save Cody a trip," Justin offered. "Plus, Cody, I didn't have your phone number. Can you share it with me? Then, if you hurry, you can make it to the tuxedo rental place and see if any adjustments need to be made on that tux."

"It's getting late."

"The tailor said as long as you make it by five thirty, she can fit you in."

Rachel watched a myriad of expressions flit across Cody's face. She could tell that he didn't want to leave her, and she wanted him to stay.

The vet assistant opened the door and called Timber's name.

Justin said, "I've got some calls to make. I'll wait for you in the car, Rachel."

"Okay."

Justin disappeared and Cody said, "I want to hear what the vet has to say. Then I'll go get fitted for the tux."

He followed Rachel and Timber through the door, and they watched as Timber obediently jumped on the examination table and allowed the vet to assess him.

"That paw is healing nicely," Dr. Levy reported. "A few more days and the slight limp will be gone as well. Timber's blood pressure, heart rate, and body temperature are all normal. I really think he's going to be fine. But the toxicology report we ran showed a sedative in his system."

"He's still not quite himself," Rachel said.

"Based on what you told me this morning, you're seeing weakness, a lack of coordination, as well as a bit of disorientation, right? Those are all side effects of the sedative. I'd be more worried if you were seeing agitation, trouble breathing, or seizures."

"Dr. Levy, would the medication you provided when you treated his paw have affected Timber the same way as the sedative—as what we're seeing now?"

"I injected anesthetic, that's all. He would have been groggy, but that would have worn off by evening, or the next morning at the very latest. The antibiotics wouldn't have caused him to slip into that deep a sleep, nor would you see lack of coordination."

"Could Timber have gone into shock?" Rachel asked.

"I doubt it. Nothing unusual happened while I was removing the glass. He actually licked my hand when he woke up. He's in top shape. Did you notice anything else unique about his behavior?"

"I don't think so." Rachel chewed her bottom lip. "I'm wondering if he's been drugged twice now—yesterday morning and yesterday evening."

"I couldn't say. But if he had two doses yesterday, then whoever gave it to him wasn't trying to kill him, just sedate him." Dr. Levy frowned. "I heard about the attack last night. Do you think someone may have drugged Timber so that he couldn't defend you?"

"We don't know," Cody said. "And we'd appreciate it if this information goes no further."

"Of course."

"If you find anything else, please call me." Cody handed the veterinarian a card from his pocket.

Timber jumped down from the examination table and followed them out of the room. Cody pulled Rachel to a stop outside the door.

"Do you think it's fair," Rachel began, "to assume that whoever attacked me last night wasn't going to kill me, and simply wanted the necklace?"

"I don't think the attacker meant to kill you last night," Cody said slowly.

Rachel wanted to feel better, to feel safe, but Cody's next words put an end to that possibility.

"That doesn't mean he won't if there's a next time."

11

"Fancy," Rachel said, after depositing Timber into the back seat of Justin's high-end vehicle. Despite the car's small size, Timber easily settled on the seat.

The seats were leather, but Justin didn't grimace at either the dog smell or wet paws. Rachel warmed a little to her future brother-in-law.

She warmed even more when he said, "I'm glad to get to spend a few minutes with you. Emily is so happy you're here. I know she'd like to build a stronger relationship with you."

"I feel the same way."

"Good to know. She's a powerhouse of energy and fun. That's what first attracted me," Justin said. "When I arrived here, she was working the front desk at the lodge. She checked me in while simultaneously hiring a housekeeper over the phone, *and* applying a fresh coat of nail polish." He chuckled. "It was the nail polish that won me over."

"Bright red?"

"With tiny pink hearts."

"That's right. You met shortly before Valentine's Day."

"Engaged two months later. I fell head over heels. I think she's the first woman I've ever truly loved." He shot a shy glance sidelong at her. "I know I'm not Emily's first love. There was Cody and, of course, Tyler before me. I can tell that all of you still get along with Cody. Did everyone get along with Tyler?"

"Yes. Why do you ask?"

Justin pulled onto the road that led to the lodge. "It's just—I get the sense that Kristin doesn't like me much, and I wondered if I don't measure up to Tyler."

Rachel hesitated, wondering how much to share. "Kristin has always been a mother hen. Tyler's been gone five years, but she's concerned Emily hasn't fully grieved him. And your relationship with Emily has happened pretty quickly."

"I know. I was willing to wait, but Emily—"

"Once Emily makes up her mind, it's a done deal. I know. Give Kristin time. She'll come around."

Pulling into the parking lot, Justin checked the time and said, "I wish I had more time to talk, but I'm scheduled for a haircut all the way in Aspen, and Emily is in the lodge dying to know if the shower is going as planned."

"The shower is on schedule and—" Rachel's phone rang, interrupting the conversation. She checked the name, and then answered. "Hello, Cody."

"Hey, Rach. Will you tell Justin that the tux fits perfectly?"

"You tell him. He's right here." Rachel handed Justin her phone and then hopped out of the car to free Timber from the back seat. Timber took off to take care of business. When she got back to the car, Justin handed her the cell back and said, "See you tonight."

Rachel entered the lodge, intending to find a towel to clean Timber's paws. Instead, Emily's voice snapped across the lobby. The check-in counter had a line and, judging by her voice, Emily was about to lose her temper. "Miss Lambert, I'm sorry for any inconvenience the theft caused you. Believe me, if we hear anything, we will contact you immediately."

Rachel stepped up next to Emily behind the counter. "I'll take over here, sis. I know you have a million things to do."

"I do," Emily said, sounding exasperated. "I just tried on my wedding slippers and the left is smaller than the right." With that, she collapsed in a chair and covered her face, letting Rachel fill in for her.

Miss Lambert didn't miss a beat. "I realize your sister's wedding is this weekend, but I must find my purse. Before I had time to cancel my debit card, the thief made some really odd purchases that the bank sent text notifications about. As if I would buy a bunch of equipment like some outdoor adventurer. I can't bear the thought of someone having my personal information. This is such a mess. I'm glad it's my last night in this rotten place." She whirled and stalked away.

Timber let out a whine, and Rachel looked past Miss Lambert's retreating form to the next couple waiting in line. "How can I help you?"

"We're here on our honeymoon," the woman gushed.

"Congratulations," Rachel said.

"I'm getting married on Saturday," Emily chimed in.

Rachel watched as Emily and the new bride bonded over their Christmas season weddings.

Then the new bride said, "Your unhappy guest won't be able to leave tomorrow. There's a snow squall on its way, with winds upward of sixty miles per hour."

"My wife's a meteorologist," the new groom said proudly.

"I didn't want to interrupt earlier," the new bride said to Emily, "but if you fill a plastic bag with water, stuff it in your shoe, and then put the shoe in the freezer for six hours, the ice will expand and your slipper might fit."

Emily perked right up. "You're kidding."

"One of my bridesmaids had the same problem and I found the fix on an online video."

Rachel slid over the room key and a piece of paper noting the Wi-Fi code. There were two more families to check in. To Rachel, working the front desk was a form of nostalgia.

"It's so great to have you back. We need you," Emily said when they no longer had an audience.

"Who's filling in tonight?"

"A high schooler from town. He's been subbing all winter, hoping we'll hire him full-time."

"Okay, I'm going to go take a shower, maybe nap for a while. I'll meet you down here in two hours."

"I'm so excited," Emily squealed. "We don't have any more check-ins today, so I'm heading to the kitchen to try the frozen-bag trick. I've got an hour to shower and dress. Justin should be here by then."

Except two hours later, Justin was a no-show. Emily was an anxious mess. "I think that meteorologist was right. It's getting colder by the second and the wind—"

"Is nothing we haven't seen before," Rachel finished for her.

"True, but he's not from here."

Another ten minutes passed with Justin not answering his phone. "Well," Emily decided, "we might as well head to the shower. Otherwise, we'll be late. Surely he'll meet us there."

Rachel shrugged into her coat, put Timber in her room, and made sure he was comfy and had everything he needed.

Once they were in Rachel's SUV, Emily said, "Justin's been so moody lately. I think he's having second thoughts."

"Not a chance," Rachel reassured her. "He told me how much he loves you when he drove me home from the vet this afternoon."

Emily's shoulders relaxed a little. "He did? Thank goodness."

"His brother isn't the most important part of the wedding," Rachel reminded her. "You are. That's what matters to Justin."

"I'm so glad you're home. Please don't stay away so long ever again. I've never forgiven myself for falling in love with Tyler."

If Rachel hadn't been driving, she'd have closed her eyes and taken a deep breath. The moment was what she had been praying for. It might hurt, but it was all for the best. She cleared her throat. "Tyler fell in love with you too. I forgave you both long ago."

It was only a beginning, but Rachel's heart began to mend as she spoke the words aloud and Emily's eyes filled with moisture.

Maybe there was still time to repair their sisterhood after all.

Cody's mother sat in the passenger seat of his Jeep, biting her lip even though she'd seen a million snowstorms. His tires slid a bit as he steered onto Main Street.

Rose gasped, gripped the grab handle with her right hand, and steadied the wedding gift on her lap with her left. "Your father thinks we should have skipped tonight and stayed home where it was safe."

"It's a ten-minute drive at most. We'll be fine, Mom."

"I have been looking forward to this shower. Emily always has such festive events. She and Justin plan on opening another lodge on the same property. Did you know that? Apparently Rocky Mountains Lodge has to refuse guests because of their limited number of rooms."

"I think Rachel mentioned that."

"Not that I can picture Justin as an innkeeper. Not like Dennis. Innkeepers don't usually drive fancy luxury vehicles. It makes the most sense for them to drive Jeeps." Rose patted the dashboard.

"I never wanted to be an innkeeper."

"I know. I remember all your dreams. There was a time you considered being a ski instructor, opening your own white-water rafting business, or—"

He laughed. "I was twelve when I had those dreams."

"And you're nearly thirty now. What is your dream now? Please tell me it's not chasing down the US Marshals' Most Wanted until you retire. I found the list. It scares me to death thinking of you coming up against criminals like that."

"Someone has to do it, Mom."

"I am proud of you—don't get me wrong. You certainly give your dad and me gray hair. But when am I going to get to attend a wedding shower for one of my sons? And—"

"Don't say it," Cody warned.

"And give me some grandchildren to spoil," she finished, exactly as he'd known she would.

He couldn't tell his mother what she wanted to hear, so he simply stopped the Jeep in front of the coffee shop, hurried around to help Rose to the front door, then parked around the corner. He noted that the lights were off in Henderson's Jewelers across the street. The police station, however, was well-lit. Cody figured he'd handed Becker more intrigue these last three days than the chief had gotten in Rolling Pine most years.

A hefty winter wind bypassed Cody's scarf and froze his cheeks. He stuffed his gloved hands in his pockets and hurried down the sidewalk. Even his knees were cold. All around him Christmas decorations promoted the season.

"Hey, Cody!" Paul and two other high school buddies pulled him through the door of Pining for Joe.

"Paul told us you were back in town," John Herbert said. "How are you doing?"

Next thing Cody knew, he'd shed his coat and was sitting at a table discussing football, the price of gas, and the crazy winds the snowstorm was supposed to bring.

"I sold out of electric heaters today," John said, coming back with two hot chocolates, each topped with a mound of whipped cream and red and green sugar sprinkles. One he passed to his wife a few tables away, and the other he kept for himself. "I'm kicking myself for not having more in stock."

"Not good for my business this close to Christmas," Paul said. "Last-minute shoppers might decide to stay home."

"Rolling Pine has weathered worse," Cody said.

"Hey." John leaned toward Cody. "I hear Rachel found some expensive jewelry at Nettie's place."

"Where did you hear that?"

"My wife. Emily was telling her about a necklace she'd be wearing at the wedding. My wife said it was worth over a hundred grand."

Cody hoped he did a better job than Paul at keeping a straight face over the exaggerated price. "You know more than I do, then," Cody responded.

"Everyone's talking," Bill Querty said, joining the table. "Mostly because you guys were in Nettie's yard with a metal detector. Do you need help looking for more jewelry?"

"What else have you found?" John asked.

Cody folded his arms on the table, leaned toward John, and said, "Nosy neighbors."

Paul laughed, and the other men joined in.

"And here's the star." Bill stood and whooped as Emily and Rachel breezed through the door. Emily hurried over to Kristin. Rachel did a round of mingling before sitting down next to her father.

Returning to his seat, Bill asked. "Where's the groom?"

"I don't see them together much," John noted. "I see Justin with Emily's mother more than I see him with Emily."

"That's because he's working for Virginia at the real estate office," Paul said. "He initially came to Rolling Pine because he was interested in land acquisition."

John finished the last of his hot chocolate with one gulp. "Well, the Andrewses have plenty of land."

"I think he's put that aside," Cody said. "It sounds like Justin and Emily are planning to build another lodge."

The conversation paused as Kate Welch came around with a tray full of cookies—little gingerbread people who sported frosting wedding veils.

"Justin's a decent guy," Bill said. "He gave me some great investment advice."

Cody tried to pay closer attention, but Rachel caught his eye—and his heart. A shimmering blue dress with gold accents highlighted her shiny black hair, and her cheeks were rosy with warmth.

To make things worse, Cody saw his mother gazing from him to Rachel and back to him again.

And smiling.

He knew that smile. It meant she knew exactly what he was thinking. Rachel had only been back in town for a couple of days, and already his mother was connecting dots between the two of them.

Someone whistled, and Cody saw Emily standing on a chair, scanning the room as she called out Justin's name.

People glanced around, but a good thirty minutes into the shower, the groom still hadn't shown up.

"If I had to guess," John said, "I'd say he's one of many drivers stuck on the side of the highway. There's no visibility thanks to the combination of snow and wind."

Cody added, "And with this wind, no doubt the cell tower's useless, so he can't call. I'll let Emily know."

Ten minutes later the door opened and Justin came in, bringing snow and wind with him, laughing as he brushed off his gloves. "Yikes. It's cold out there."

Emily didn't seem to care. She was in his arms and then helping him with his coat, touching his hair. "Hey, you didn't get a haircut."

"I was halfway there when I realized the weather wasn't cooperating, so I turned around. Took me three times as long to get back."

Settling back in his chair, Cody watched the comings and goings of the townspeople. His mother and Rachel's mother were off at a table whispering—no doubt about grandchildren. Bob Lewis was in the corner trying to convince Stuart Welch that Biggles should be allowed in the room. Stuart, out of concern for Biggles, had put a blanket and some food in the employee bathroom for the dog. Kristin was busy taking pictures. And Chris Mack was on his knees working to stabilize one of the tables that was off-balance.

Cookies and mugs of hot chocolate adorned every table as the guests played games. Cody won a coffee maker by unscrambling fifty words that had to do with being married.

"And you're not even married," Paul teased.

"I took a code-breaking class," Cody said modestly. "It probably gave me a huge advantage."

Bill and John took off to find their wives.

Paul leaned forward and whispered, "I didn't tell a soul about the jewelry, not even my wife. How does everyone know?"

"Between Emily and the necklace and seeing us searching Nettie's front yard, someone put two and two together and spread the word around town."

"What are you going to do?"

"Nothing." What Cody wanted to say was, "Double the effort to find the stolen earring," but suddenly he was worried about who might hear him. Something was wrong in Rolling Pine. Someone wasn't who they claimed to be. Paul had mentioned his father was spending lots of money trying to find George. How much did a small-town jeweler make?

How worried about finances was Paul, really? Suddenly, everyone was suspicious.

Rachel joined Paul and Cody. Her cheeks were flushed from playing hostess, and Cody wanted to brush a strand of hair away from her face but stopped himself.

It had been less than a week, and he'd never been one to act on impulse. Oh, but how he wanted to.

"This is fun," she said brightly. "The games went so well. How cool that you won a coffee maker."

Cody cleared his throat. "Does Emily need a coffee maker?"

She laughed. "We live in a lodge. We have enough coffee makers."

"You live in Arizona," Cody reminded her in a tone that came out frostier than he'd intended. "How about there?"

"Thanks, but I already have one." Rachel twisted away to watch her sister open presents, and his side suddenly felt cold.

Cody slipped the box under his chair and watched Emily open another present—a coffee maker.

"It's okay," Rachel murmured to him. "If she and Justin open another lodge, they'll need one for each of the guest rooms."

Emily picked up a plastic bag from Herbert's Outdoor Outfitters, and Bob Lewis called, "That's from me. Sorry, I didn't have any wrapping paper."

"It's all right, Bob." Justin was gathering up gift wrapping and tossing it into a recycling bag. "Less for me to throw away."

From the Herberts' bag, Emily pulled a square blue velvet box. She opened it and gasped as she pulled out a bracelet. "It's beautiful."

"It is, isn't it?" Bob said, beaming with pride.

Cody half-rose before Paul tugged him back to his seat.

Emily thanked Bob, then she came over to show Rachel. Paul and Cody leaned in to study the piece. It was structured like three separate bracelets linked as one, the stones sparkling as diamonds should, but strangely dark in color.

"Isn't it awesome?" Emily gushed before hurrying over to Justin. He made a big deal out of it.

Cody stretched across the aisle and asked Bob, "Was that a family heirloom?"

"No," Bob said.

"Where did you find it?"

"Never lost it."

Cody told himself that it was not the time or place to question Bob further. Too many ears, too little privacy.

The party returned to full swing, nobody apparently noticing that one table no longer joined in the festivities. "Paul?" Cody asked quietly. "Could you tell anything from that quick assessment?"

"I'd need my loupe to be sure, but I think the stones were diamonds set over obsidian. They sure look real. If so, it would be expensive, for sure."

"She'll have to give it back," Rachel said. "It's too much."

"Yes," Cody agreed. "But give it back to whom? I could be wrong, but I very much doubt that it really belongs to Bob."

12

*T*he wind howled as Cody carried yet another armload of presents from the coffee shop to Dennis's van. Rachel, Justin, and Dennis followed carrying more gifts.

"Only my daughter," Dennis joked through chattering teeth, "would consider December a prime wedding month."

Either his comment wasn't funny or, like Cody, everyone was too busy fighting the cold to comment.

They made three more trips.

"I'll put these in the trunk of my car." Justin held up the last few bags. "Emily wants to get back to the lodge. She has some ideas to write down."

No one protested. Cody followed Rachel to her SUV and waited until she got in before going around to the passenger side. They sat in silence for a few moments, shivering, waiting for the heat to penetrate the vehicle. Finally, he unwound his scarf, pushed back his hood, and asked, "Did you see Bob leave?"

Rachel shed a layer as well. "Dr. Levy drove him and Biggles home. Justin offered, but Emily wanted him to do something. Now, are you going to tell me what was going on in there concerning Emily's bracelet?"

"Right now, it's nothing but speculation on my part."

"I already know it's not an Ankar. I researched that on my phone and it seems Ankar creations do not include obsidian. And I know that more than anything, you'd like to know how Bob wound up with it.

So I guess what I'm really asking, Cody, is what's going on in Rolling Pine, and why is all this expensive jewelry suddenly popping up all over the place?"

Instead of answering, he posed his own question. "What are you doing tomorrow?"

She gave him a look that he recognized as pure annoyance. He wasn't telling her everything, and she didn't like the secrets, especially since they involved her. "I'll be at Grandma Nettie's most of the day, either shoveling, searching for the missing earring, or dealing with repairs. You didn't answer my question."

"Believe me, I want to know why all this jewelry is popping up just as much as you do."

And none of it, so far, relating back to Hammonds.

"We need to get this new bracelet to Paul," Cody said. "Then we need to head over to Bob's and ask some important questions."

"I do want to hear what he has to say."

"And we need to get busy hunting for the other earring. John Herbert was asking about the jewelry that's been found on your grandmother's property. He doesn't know details, but he knows it's worth a lot."

"You're kidding."

"I'm not." Cody put his scarf back on, then opened the door and got out, his breath wisping in the air, snowflakes settling in his hair. He stared at her a moment, not wanting to leave her. What was she thinking?

Finally, he closed the door and stepped back.

Rachel put the SUV in gear and it slid backward for a second before catching traction. She headed out of the coffee shop parking lot and down the snow-flanked street.

He watched her, wishing he was sitting next to her.

His phone rang, and he answered. "What do you have, Chief?"

"I came across some interesting tidbits today. I was nosing around, trying to locate the purse Lydia Lambert is so worried about," Chief Becker said. "I talked to Elmore Banks, who tried to give me a puppy, but also mentioned that he'd seen Miss Lambert driving out near Bob Lewis's place. Then I happened to go into the Main Street Fashion Center. When I asked if they'd found any purses, I discovered Miss Lambert had already been there, but not for a purse. For a necklace. One of the cashiers saw her walk into Henderson's Jewelers after that."

"Interesting," Cody agreed, hurrying toward his Jeep.

"Here's something else. Emily said that Lydia Lambert was upset about a charge on her credit card. I believe Lambert said 'as if I were some outdoor adventurer.' It got me thinking, so I went to Herbert's Outdoor Outfitters and asked if they'd been contacted about any fraudulent purchases. They hadn't. Then I asked if Lydia Lambert had been a recent customer."

"What did they say?"

"John didn't remember seeing her, but that he had a receipt with her name on it for purchasing a metal detector."

"What?"

"The purchase happened after Miss Lambert reported her purse missing. And I watched the security camera footage. I didn't see her, but there sure were a lot of bundled-up people. Here's where it gets weird. John said that Miss Lambert occasionally came in and made purchases, but always in cash, never with a card."

Disconnecting the call, all Cody could think was that something wasn't right. What was Lydia Lambert searching for? And why report her purse and credit cards stolen if they hadn't been?

Then Cody frowned. He wasn't putting Rachel's safety first.

He threw open the door of his Jeep and jumped in, alarm growing.

He needed to keep Rachel in his sights. Cody was relieved when he caught up with her a few blocks later, and he followed her to the lodge.

The US Marshal motto had to do with justice, integrity, and service. And Cody was certain that Rachel needed his professional protection. She'd witnessed a man in a black coat, carrying a gun, leaving the scene of an explosion on her grandmother's property.

The problem was that Cody knew he wasn't protecting Rachel because of his job. He was protecting her because he cared for her.

And Cody knew from his training that the heart got in the way when someone was in danger. He had to be rational, put his feelings aside, and do his job. Which meant ensuring that Rachel made it safely to her living quarters.

After doing so, Cody headed for the front desk—only to be informed that Lydia Lambert had checked out.

On Wednesday morning, Rachel woke before her alarm. Dressing quickly, she looked out the window at a winter wonderland. The storm had passed, leaving great drifts of snow and a few downed trees.

Timber pranced at her side. He followed her to the back door and hurried out to do his business before coming back in. She toweled him off and then headed for the kitchen. Kristin sat at the table with her laptop open, a true-crime documentary on the screen, coffee in hand.

"You always did like mysteries." Rachel peered over Kristin's shoulder and watched for a few moments.

"This series is my favorite. They have a new broadcast every Wednesday. Did you know that a decades-old cold case happened right here in Colorado, and was solved using genetic genealogy? I find it amazing." Her voice softened. "I think a lot about how crimes are solved, mostly because I feel like I'm living in some sort of holding pattern."

"Because of George?"

"That's right. My favorite podcast always ends with a hopeful spin and a call out to anyone who might know more information. It makes me think that somewhere, somebody knows what happened to George, and there's still hope that I might find him. Even if it's not the way I'd want, finding him at all would offer some closure, and perhaps then I could begin to move forward."

Rachel squeezed Kristin's shoulder. "I believe there's still hope that you'll solve this mystery."

"What mystery?" Justin asked as he came into the room.

Instead of answering, Kristin closed the podcast and brought up another screen. "We've had two cancellations due to the weather."

Rachel poured herself a cup of coffee, topped off Kristin's, and sat across from her at the table. "Do you think any of the guests will want to leave?"

Kristin closed her laptop. "Probably not. This also means some of Emily's out-of-state friends might not be able to make it to the wedding. What about your friends, Justin?"

"Not coming. They called this morning."

"Are you going to tell Emily?"

"Not a chance." With that, Justin took his coffee and exited the room.

"It's always amazed me how the weather can change so quickly. The sun's out this morning, and there are still two days for the roads to clear," Rachel pointed out. "People will show up. We Coloradans are a hardy bunch."

"I don't know," Kristin said doubtfully. "This wedding's not going as smoothly as the first. First, the explosion, then you find expensive jewelry in your grandma's yard, the best man bails, you're attacked, and now Bob is giving Emily expensive jewelry too. When Emily married Tyler, Bob gave her a paper towel holder circa 1950."

"What makes you think the bracelet Bob gave to Emily was expensive?" Rachel asked.

"Well, I was watching Paul's face when Emily showed it to you and Cody. He's a jeweler, so I figured if his eyes went that wide over it, the bracelet probably isn't costume."

"Well, it was an unusual gift." Rachel bit her lip.

Kristin raised an eyebrow.

Emily walked into the room. "What was an unusual gift?"

"The bracelet Bob gave you," Rachel said.

"I know. When I married Tyler, Bob gave me a paper towel holder."

Kristin elbowed Emily, who blanched.

"It's okay," Rachel hurried to interject. "You can say Tyler's name all you want."

Emily nodded. "Thank you. It helps me to talk about him."

"Do you mind if I take your new bracelet to Paul this morning and ask him to appraise it?" Rachel asked.

"Go ahead. I'd like to know too. I would come with you but I'm scheduled to meet with the minister this morning."

"Thanks. Where are you keeping it?" Rachel asked.

"Justin put it in the safe last night." Emily led the way out the door. "Have you seen him this morning?"

"He was here a little bit ago."

"I hope he remembers about the minister. He missed the last session."

Together, the women left the family quarters and entered the main part of the lodge. Timber followed at Rachel's feet, stopping every so often to sniff at something.

Rachel glanced around the lobby. Her father had been born and raised there. Her great-grandfather had built it as a rustic bed-and-breakfast with only four rooms to let. He'd wanted a way to earn money and had been a wise man.

That morning, the lobby was filled with wreaths and her mother's Santa Claus collection. Two giant Nutcrackers flanked the fireplace. Cinnamon- and apple-scented candles gave the room a rich ambience.

Kristin headed behind the counter, bending to open a cabinet door to reveal the safe. She took a ring of keys from her pocket and unlocked a drawer from which she removed yet another key. Before she could open the safe, the phone rang, and she stepped toward the desk to answer.

While Rachel waited, she watched a few guests milling about a sitting area. Over the years, the lodge's original four rooms had grown into family quarters while three generations of Andrewses had expanded the lodge into a cozy retreat for tourists.

The fireplace took up one wall. That was Grandfather's doing. Floor-to-ceiling windows on each side of it looked out on the Arapahoe National Forest, which was her father's doing. He loved a good view. A custom chandelier—a first-year wedding anniversary gift from Tyler to Emily—hung at the center of the high-vaulted ceiling. It had been too big for the small apartment they shared above the lodge's garage. Emily had always considered the lodge her home.

And now Emily and Justin would make their mark by constructing a whole new building.

Kristin finally got off the phone and finished opening the safe, bringing out the box containing Emily's bracelet. She handed it to Rachel.

"Don't lose it," Emily warned. "I like it more than the necklace. It's striking, rather than classic."

A guest came down the stairs, asking if the restaurant was open. Rachel carried the bracelet back to her room, hurried into her winter attire, and zipped the blue box into the same coat pocket in which she'd stored the Ankar bracelet after finding it in the snow. She started her car remotely before trekking outside. Timber bounded a few steps ahead of her, ready to go. He dashed around and rolled in the snow while she turned on the defroster and then scraped the windows.

Her dad came out to help. "You and Cody seemed comfortable last night," he remarked.

"Old friends often do, Dad."

Finally, her fingers frozen even though she wore gloves, Rachel and her father finished with the windows, and she and Timber were able to drive into town, slipping and sliding for much of the way.

Few cars were parked in front of the Pine Derby Restaurant. She pulled in next to Cody's Jeep and took Timber in with her. If it had been crowded, more than likely someone would claim annoyance at having a dog in the restaurant. Normally, it wasn't an issue because Timber was either working—making him a service dog—or they were in a place with an outside patio.

Timber shook the dampness from his coat. Rachel thought about asking for a towel, but the mat by the front door absorbed all the melted snow. She scanned the room until she saw Cody drinking coffee and scrolling through a tablet. She walked over to join him.

"Learn anything new?" she asked, glancing at the specials listed on a dry erase board over the cashier stand.

"It was a killer storm last night—downed trees, collapsed roofs, and they're still clearing the highway."

A waitress came by, poured coffee for Rachel, and took their orders.

"I was the first vehicle out of the lodge's parking lot this morning, except for the plow," Rachel said. "I slid more than drove. It's been a while since I've driven in these conditions."

"You should have called me. I'd have come and gotten you."

"I'm fine," Rachel insisted. "I'm just eager to get to Grandma Nettie's place. Chris told me last night that he'd gone over and covered all the exposed areas with plywood, but I worried all night anyway."

"I drove by this morning. I could see where he'd shored things up. Everything was fine."

"That makes me feel better."

"Good. Did you grab your dad's metal detector?" Cody asked.

"I have Emily's bracelet, but no, I didn't bring the detector, not with this kind of snow cover. I'm not even sure what Justin did with it."

"It doesn't hurt to try. I have Paul's metal detector in the Jeep." Cody went back to his tablet.

Rachel took out her phone. She was behind on responding to texts, but it sounded like her business in Arizona was surviving without her. The waitress refilled their coffee and set a bowl of water on the floor for Timber. Then Rachel got to her newest text, which was from Kristin.

She froze and let out an unintentional "Oh."

Cody leaned over and tried to see. "What's wrong?"

"Nothing." She moved the phone so he couldn't see the screen.

Amidst the myriad wedding shower photos that Kristin had sent, one in particular stood out—Rachel and Cody at a small table with their heads bent close together over the bracelet in Emily's hand.

Only Cody and Rachel weren't looking at the bracelet. They were looking at each other.

Who else besides Kristin and her dad had noticed what had clearly been more than camaraderie?

Rachel met Cody's gaze. His eyes asked a question she couldn't interpret. Or maybe she didn't want to.

Never mind the picture.

Powering off her phone, she set it facedown as the waitress arrived with their food.

"Photos from last night?" he asked. "Can I see?"

"Sorry, I've shut off my phone so we wouldn't be interrupted."

"Too bad. Emily and Justin were obviously having a good time," Cody remarked, picking up his fork.

Rachel ate quickly, as if shoveling down food would somehow keep the moment from feeling awkward. It didn't.

He stopped eating.

"What?" She put down her fork.

"Rachel, I don't want to bring up bad memories, but what happened? How did Emily wind up with Tyler, the boyfriend *you* brought home from college?"

No one had ever asked her that question except Grandma Nettie. Her mother had tried once, but the pain in Virginia's eyes had ensured that Rachel would never share the truth.

Alone in the Pine Derby Restaurant felt like a strange situation for unburdening, but maybe it was time. Rachel's plate was empty, so she pushed it away and began. "I brought Tyler home over winter break for two whole weeks. I'd already met his family."

"So you were getting serious?"

"Very. Tyler and I had a lot of common interests. We hiked a lot and had joined a racquetball club. We liked to binge-watch television from the sixties. We competed when our favorite trivia game show was on, kept track of our scores, and at the end of the week, the loser had to take the winner out for pizza."

"I love pizza."

She knew that as well as she knew what he was doing—trying to help her keep it light. "Tyler could hardly wait to meet my family, get to know everyone, and try skiing."

"Was he any good?"

She gave a strangled laugh. "No, he was terrible. Emily and I took him to Aspen Mountain. The first time we took him, he stayed at the bottom of the hill for hours. He'd force his way up an incline about two or three yards, then he'd fall. We went back the next day and that time, he made it to the ski lift. But when the lift chair came, instead of hopping on, he fell on his face with his skis sticking in the air. They had to stop the lift."

"They never stop the lift."

"It's rare." Rachel giggled.

"Did he ever make it to the top?"

"Eventually. Two instructors lifted him onto a chair, and off into the air he went."

"Good."

She shook her head. "Actually it was bad. He left his poles behind."

One side of Cody's mouth twitched. "Those are pretty important for the exit."

She grinned. "The good news is that when he fell that time, he didn't interfere with the lift."

Cody laughed.

After a moment, Rachel did too. "Tyler didn't mind making mistakes, failing when he took risks. He'd always try again. Over that Christmas break, eventually, he made it down the bunny hill. We went skiing about five more times. He and Emily did the bunny hill over and over, and I skied the other slopes by myself. It didn't bother me a bit. I wanted him to connect with my family."

Cody pushed his empty plate aside, and took a long sip of coffee.

"It was great. My family loved him. He jumped right in and helped out at the lodge, carried luggage for guests, learned how to check people in. We went out to eat, drove to Vail and Aspen for events, and he knew to let Grandma Nettie win at checkers."

"Smart man," Cody agreed.

"Anyway, we went back to college and things seemed like they were good. He was a year ahead of me, so he graduated that May, and we came back to the Rocky Mountains Lodge after finals. He began working for my dad, and I went back to school for summer classes. I missed him something fierce. I started thinking maybe I'd transfer and do my last year at Boulder."

"But you didn't."

"No, I came home after my classes ended. In truth, I knew something was off during our phone calls. They went from an hour each evening to twenty minutes, to sometimes five. It was like he had nothing to share. When I came back home and walked through the lodge's front door, the way he hugged me—I just knew."

"But did you know it was Emily?"

"Not yet."

"Did he tell you?"

"He did. That first evening we hiked the forest, all the way to Grandma Nettie's house. He'd already told Emily that he'd fallen in love with her and that he was breaking it off with me. He loved me, but not the way he loved Emily. In the last mile of that hike, I heard the sorrow in his voice from hurting me, but I also heard a joy that couldn't be denied. I couldn't stand in their way."

"And he left you with Nettie."

"He did. It helped with my heartbreak, in a way. My parents already knew, and Emily threatened to elope if they interfered. Mom was upset. It took Dad a long time to forgive Tyler."

"How did you cope?"

"I went back to school and threw myself into my studies. I'd never had such good grades. After I graduated, I stayed. I only came home when I absolutely had to. Eventually, it didn't bother me so much. I got over him. The distance helped. I found a haven in Arizona, loved my job and friends, made a life. I eventually got over it, but Emily couldn't handle being around me."

"Why?"

"Guilt, maybe. I don't know. Tyler clearly adored her. I was no threat to their happiness. Then, when he got into that accident, it felt too late to make amends. She was busy piecing her heart back together, and she didn't want my help."

"So, maybe now with Justin, you two will have a second chance?"

She managed a smile. "Already working on it."

He reached across the table and put his hand on hers. "I'm glad."

Rachel wondered if Cody would still be glad if he discovered how she felt about him. Would he pull his hand away in surprise? Or would he wrap his fingers around hers and tell her that he felt the same?

Until she found the courage to share what was in her heart, whether or not Cody returned her feelings would remain another mystery.

13

Cody took her arm as they crossed the street to Paul's jewelry shop.

Paul met them at the door, holding it open and ushering them in before a gust of wind could follow.

Rachel unzipped her pocket, pulled out the blue box, and handed it to Paul. "Is it okay if I bring Timber in? He's very well behaved and won't disturb your merchandise."

"I have two dogs," Paul said. "Doesn't bother me."

In less than a minute, he had flipped on the lights, ratcheted up the heat, and stood behind the counter laying out the familiar velvety purple cloth. Next, he took a small light and his loupe from a desk behind him, then began his examination.

Timber settled on the floor. Rachel took a rubber collapsible bowl from her bag and made sure Timber had water before she joined Cody and Paul to take some photos.

"Hmmm," Paul murmured a moment later, sounding surprised. "It's gray obsidian. In the coffee shop last night, I thought it was black." Paul frowned at them. "Are you sure it's the same bracelet?"

"Justin put it in the safe last night, and then I took it out this morning," Rachel said.

"If it's real, I'd say eighteen karat, with diamonds of various qualities. I'm sorry to say I don't recognize the designer. I can put out some feelers if you'd like. If it's not real, it's an excellent fake."

"Let me use my contacts first," Cody said.

Paul raised an eyebrow, clearly hoping for a different response.

Cody hadn't shared any case specifics with Paul. The US Marshals often relied on informants, but Paul and Rachel were not informants, and they knew nothing about Richard Hammonds.

And Cody wasn't entirely certain that Paul could be trusted with details. After discovering that the whole town knew about the suspicious jewelry, Cody had begun to consider Paul a person of interest.

In addition to which, there was another person who had become a person of interest.

"What did Lydia Lambert purchase from you the other day?" Cody asked.

"Why are you asking about Lydia Lambert?" Rachel said.

"Chief Becker called me late last night. He's been trying to locate her purse and instead stumbled upon some odd behavior. What I'm trying to figure out is whether Lydia Lambert bought a metal detector, or if someone else did, using her stolen credit card. Chief Becker will compare her signature on the charge with her signature in Paul's ledger here. Lydia has also been going into businesses and asking to go through their lost and found items, saying something about a missing necklace."

"You think Miss Lambert has something to do with the mysterious jewelry floating around town?" Rachel asked.

"She acted a bit dramatic over the missing purse. Becker became suspicious. And if Paul's questioning the legitimacy of this bracelet, we need to find out what time the bracelet was locked up and what time Miss Lambert checked out."

"She comes in fairly often to check my consignment display," Paul said.

"Does she ever buy anything?"

"Yes, and she's got a good eye. She bought a pair of earrings that I'd verified, and she was quite excited about the find."

"Do you have a copy of the receipt?"

"Sure," Paul said. "But she paid with cash."

People who didn't want to leave a trail paid with cash. Cody turned to Rachel. "Would you mind calling the lodge for me to get Miss Lambert's contact information?"

"I'll call Kristin. She can probably answer any questions we might have."

Kristin answered on the first ring. In under a minute, Rachel was sharing Lambert's address in a city Cody had never heard of. A phone number, as well as her vehicle's make, model, and license plate number followed. "Kristin says it's a rented four-door sedan with fairly new snow tires."

"Ask her if Miss Lambert paid for her stay at the lodge in cash."

Rachel relayed the question, then nodded to him, and Cody typed a few more words into an email on his phone before hitting *Send*. He wanted a history on Lydia Lambert, who evidently hailed from Persistent, Idaho.

Rachel wore a funny expression when she disconnected.

"What?" Cody asked.

"Kristin said that Lydia checked out sometime last night."

"Yes, that bothers me too. Paul, can I see your consignment pieces?"

Paul led him to a display case by the entrance. Cody had walked past it a dozen times, barely noticing, but he took his time to examine the pieces closely. Lydia Lambert was asking around about a necklace, both Emily and Rachel had unexpectedly come into some very expensive jewelry, and Cody was hunting for a jewel thief.

"How often do people bring you items on consignment?" Cody asked.

"Not too often. Usually people try to consign junk."

"So it's rare to consign quality pieces?"

"Serious pieces would fetch more in Aspen or Denver. They deal with that kind of money. We don't."

"Did anyone else come in here asking questions or searching for something a little out of the ordinary?" Cody asked.

"Until you showed up, I felt like I was living in Mayberry."

"Welcome to the latest episode of Rolling Pine 911," Cody joked. "Now, let's check on that bracelet Rachel found yesterday that we gave you to lock up."

Paul was gone less than a minute before they heard him shout. Cody, with Rachel and Timber at his heels, burst through the door separating the store from the office and found Paul on his knees. He quickly stood, holding the Ankar bracelet in his hand. With his foot, he pushed the safe's door shut. "Look!"

Cody assessed a few important details. The Hendersons had chosen their safe wisely. It was a combination-lock safe secured to the ground with anchor bolts and a thick door, all surrounded by a hardened steel plate.

"Is that a bullet hole?" Rachel leaned closer.

"It's from a drill," Cody said.

"And only one hole," Paul noted. "Very few scratch marks."

"Something, or someone, interrupted the thief," Cody said, "before he finished cracking the safe."

While Paul called Chief Becker, Cody watched Rachel pace the store, pausing every so often to peer outside. Timber, ever alert, mimicked his owner.

When Cody came to stand beside her, she whirled on him. "The thief wanted the Ankar bracelet from the safe?"

"That would be my guess. And Paul mentioned to me once that this store has automatic door locks. With the storm that blew through last night, it's quite possible that the locks and the security alarm and cameras were disabled."

"And whoever tried to break into the safe is probably the same person who stole the earring from my room."

"Possibly. Was Lydia Lambert a guest at your lodge at the time your earring was switched out for a fake?"

"Yes."

Cody let out his breath. *Far-fetched? Yes. Impossible? No.* "Right now," he said, "I'm wondering why Lydia Lambert was really in Rolling Pine."

"She sure doesn't fit the picture of what I imagine when I think of a jewel thief," Rachel said.

"It doesn't take strength to break into a safe. It takes patience and the right tools."

Before he had time to say anything further, the front door pushed open. Cold air swirled in behind Chief Becker, who was snapping orders into his radio. "Go ahead and barricade the area. Check the side roads and see if anyone's stuck."

Ending the call, he said, "Last night's storm caused a mess. People without services. Road closures. Downed trees." He headed to the back with Cody and Rachel following behind.

"Stay," Rachel ordered Timber, who whined a little but obeyed.

Chief Becker knelt to study the marks on the safe. "The thief gave it a good shot with a drill, but didn't have the right tools to break all the way in. Good on the Hendersons for choosing such a tough safe." He scribbled in a small notebook and asked Paul a few questions.

Paul reiterated that nothing was missing, grumbled something about the door locks and video cameras not working, and then left to call his insurance company and a locksmith.

Quickly, Cody filled Becker in on the bracelet Emily had received at her shower and why they had brought it to Paul, plus their mounting suspicions about Lydia Lambert.

"Not much I can do until we clean up the mess from the storm," the chief said. "I'll cordon off the area and be back as soon as I can."

"Chief, Paul had a few things to add about Lydia Lambert."

Chief Becker raised an eyebrow.

Cody continued. "Paul says she's been in here often, scrutinizing the consignment jewelry. I got to thinking that maybe her purse wasn't stolen. Maybe that whole act was a ploy to get people thinking she was a victim."

"Stranger things have happened," Becker said. "But she's been coming here for a few years and hasn't caused any trouble except being a bit annoying—until this thing with the purse. The first couple of times she came to town, she'd visit the station with a photo of a woman, wanting to know if I'd seen the woman in the photo around Rolling Pine."

"Had you?"

"No."

"Do you remember the woman's name?" Cody asked.

"When I get back to the station, I'll check my notes. But, while I don't remember the name, I do remember investigating Lambert's claim. The woman Miss Lambert was searching for had been reported missing many times before."

Cody had a few notes of his own to check. He pulled out his tablet to see if he had received any updates on Lydia Lambert.

He read his email twice before saying, "Lydia Lambert—at least the one staying at the Rocky Mountains Lodge—does not exist."

It was noon when Rachel and Cody finally left Henderson's Jewelers. She squinted against the sun as she let Timber into the back of Cody's Jeep, then climbed into the passenger side.

"What's next?" she asked Cody.

"Heading to Bob's place to see where he came across the bracelet and if he's turned up any additional jewelry."

"Okay."

"Then we'll head to Nettie's and look for the missing earring."

"I hope we find it fast," Rachel said. "I want to get back to the lodge and ask Kristin if she remembers Miss Lambert asking about a missing person. Kristin might know the name of the woman in Miss Lambert's photo."

"Of course. But please let me ask the questions."

"That's no fun. Meanwhile, how about I listen while you tell me everything that's going on?" Rachel suggested. "From the beginning."

Cody started the Jeep and pulled onto the almost-deserted street. Rachel stared out the window at the businesses, noting that most were open despite the storm.

"I've already mentioned that I'm a US Marshal in town for a case." Cody reached into his coat pocket, withdrew a badge, and handed it to her.

She pulled off a glove and fingered the simple identification. The top, in capital letters, read *United States*. The bottom read *Marshal*. The center star was adorned by an eagle and a tiny American flag.

"I'm impressed. It's not easy to make it through the Marshal academy. I've worked with a few Marshals during search and rescue missions. They've always gone above and beyond."

"That's part of the reason I joined," Cody said. "I'm still relatively new, so I'm usually assigned to light duty and backup. It surprised me when I asked for time off to attend Emily's wedding in Rolling Pine and received all kinds of attention. It seems our little hometown had been on my superiors' radar because they'd received an anonymous tip that a fugitive might be in this area."

"The jewelry thief you mentioned?" Rachel guessed.

"Yes. We've been calling him Richard Hammonds."

"And have you made a connection between the jewelry you found at Grandma Nettie's and any jewelry taken by Hammonds?"

"No. I've done detailed comparisons as well as sent photos to my superiors. No similarities yet."

"So my jewelry and the jewelry taken by Hammonds might not be related?"

"So far, I can't find a clear connection."

"But you're trying to find one. Since I arrived, you've been by my side through one incident after another, keeping me safe."

"Just doing my job."

Rachel was surprised to feel wounded by his words. She'd been about to tell him that she was starting to get used to his company, about to admit that she liked being with him, and that together they would figure out the puzzle. But if the time he'd spent with her was simply because of his job, then maybe it would be better to keep her budding affection to herself.

Cody steered down a road that Chief Becker probably should have barricaded. Rachel must have made a face because Cody said, "Don't worry. The Jeep has plenty of ground clearance, and I can always add more traction. Any other vehicle and we'd be doing this after the snow melts."

Clearing her throat, Rachel asked, "Why doesn't anyone know you're a Marshal? Why are you keeping it a secret? My parents don't know. Emily doesn't know. I haven't heard any rumors in town."

He took a moment to answer. "It's not that I was keeping it a secret," he said slowly. "At first, I didn't share because I was afraid of failing at a job I really love."

"Have you ever failed at anything you really wanted?"

"Maybe once," he laughed.

"And what was that?"

"A relationship," he admitted.

Before Rachel had the chance to ask questions that she might have regretted, Cody pulled to the side of the road and parked.

Rachel hesitated before getting out. "I don't think this driveway's ever been touched by a shovel."

"Makes sense. Bob doesn't drive." Cody checked his phone, released his seat belt, and opened his door.

Rachel stumbled into the snow and freed Timber from the back seat before attempting to step into the trail Cody's footprints had blazed. Finally, he reached back to take her arm, and together they slogged through snow that hit the top of their boots.

"Biggles isn't barking," Cody noted.

"That could mean that Bob isn't home. He's always been a wanderer." She hadn't been to Bob's place in a long time, but she remembered visiting him with her dad to bring leftover food.

Cody knocked, waited, and knocked again. On his third attempt, he pounded harder and the door swung open. He frowned, pushed the door all the way open, and stepped inside.

Rachel stamped the snow from her boots and followed him in.

Her boot slipped a bit, and Cody once again took her arm to steady her. They scanned a rather messy living area.

"You don't think Bob would leave it like this, do you?" she asked.

"I would hope not."

It was an older mobile home with an olive-green and burnt-orange interior. A bed was tucked in the far corner with its sheets pulled back and a pillow had been tossed to the floor. A gun rack was mounted on the wall with enough slots for four rifles, but Bob only had one. Cupboard doors hung open with the contents strewn on the floor and counters. Dirty dishes were piled on the table and in the sink.

Biggles's water dish was full, slightly frozen over, and his food bowl was also full. Cody headed for the open bathroom door, and Rachel could see that it was a mess in there too.

Cody strode across to the front door. "We need to check the cabin as well."

When they stepped back out of the mobile home, cold bit at Rachel's cheeks until she rewrapped her scarf. Timber stayed by her side, undaunted by the temperature. They reached the old cabin with a *Condemned* sign in the window. The front porch creaked when Cody stepped on it. He hesitated, and Rachel worried that the floorboard would give and he'd disappear from sight.

Like the mobile home, the cabin's door wasn't locked.

Rachel knew that at one time a whole family had lived in the one-room building. An old mattress sagged against one wall. An antique black stove stood against another wall. Wind whistled through parts of the home where chinking had worn away between the logs.

Timber came in, sniffed around, found the place uninteresting, and went back outside.

Since Bob clearly wasn't there, Rachel followed her dog. She stopped so abruptly that Cody bumped into her.

"What?"

"Timber's alerting."

Cody scanned the swells of unbroken snow. "Is there something out there?"

"Not that I can see. Last time he did this was behind Grandma Nettie's when the water heater blew and I saw someone running away."

Cody walked toward her dog, a good ten or twelve yards through heavy snow, his head swiveling right, left, forward, as he searched for any signs of disturbance.

After a moment, Cody returned. "I don't see a thing."

Rachel called Timber, and he happily bounded toward her. She rubbed him behind the ears and gave him a treat from the bag she kept in her pocket.

When they got back to Cody's Jeep, Rachel listened while Cody called Chief Becker about Timber's alert. He also asked the chief to be on the lookout for Bob.

Ending the call, Cody started the vehicle and told Rachel, "Becker says he'll come out here as soon as he deals with a house fire. In the meantime, he'll have an officer check Bob's regular haunts and make a few calls. When it's too cold, Bob often heads to either the library or the vet's office."

"Good to know."

Rachel settled back in her seat, happy to enjoy the warmth coming from the heater for a few miles, and thinking about hot chocolate from Grandma Nettie's kitchen. She wanted to check that the tarp was still holding strong too.

When they arrived in her grandmother's neighborhood, Cody's father, William, was shoveling a neighbor's sidewalk. Cody pulled up alongside. "Hi, Dad. Good to see you. How was your trip?"

"Boring compared to what's been going on around here. Chief Becker called to ask us to keep an eye out for Bob. Did you find him yet?"

"No."

"Be careful over at Nettie's," William warned. "There are more than a few trees that took a tumble last night."

Before Cody could restart the Jeep, a stream of children passed in front of them.

"That was us not so long ago," Cody said, pointing out his window as three little kids—all on one snow disc—slid down a driveway and crashed into a parked car that probably belonged to their unsuspecting parents.

"I never ran into a parked car," Rachel said.

"No, you preferred driving snowmobiles into the river."

Rachel punched him in the arm. "That happened once, yet somehow I'll never live it down."

Cody parked in Grandma Nettie's driveway. Icicles, some as long as two feet, hung from the gutters, dripping onto the snow and sidewalk.

"I'll start shoveling the walk," Cody said. "Shouldn't take long. Why don't you go inside and check things out?"

Timber elected to stay with Cody. Rachel went into the house, noting the chill and missing the days when there would be a fire in the fireplace.

She set water to boil on the gas stove and found hot chocolate packets in the cabinet. Then she headed to the spare bedroom where she and Emily had stayed during their sleepovers. Thick socks were in the top drawer, and Rachel quickly changed into them. By the time she had her boots back on, the water was boiling.

She called Cody in. Five minutes later, they both had warm stomachs and a plan.

"Let's concentrate on the back today."

"Sounds like a good idea," Rachel agreed.

Cody wasn't quite finished shoveling the walk out front, so Rachel headed out by herself. She used her shovel for balance as she and Timber walked from Grandma Nettie's back porch toward the edge of her grandmother's property that bordered the Arapahoe National Forest. The storm had left downed limbs and one overturned tree. It wasn't often that an entire tree fell, at least behind Grandma's. Rachel could only remember it happening one other time, and Grandma Nettie had explained that structural imbalance or root problems put trees at risk.

Rachel found a somewhat bare spot and started sifting with her shovel, turning over stones, small twigs, and hard mud.

What would Grandma Nettie make of all this? If she were there now, she might have told Rachel that everything was okay and there was a logical explanation for the Ankar jewelry.

Grandma Nettie would also listen if Rachel was willing to open up about her feelings for Cody—feelings that had always been there but were buried deep because of Emily, like the earring they were searching for.

Rachel's fingers hurt and her cheeks were numb. Melting snow trickled down her boots, and her fresh socks were growing damp. About the time she was determined to stop, Timber made an odd sound. He stood in front of a fallen tree, alerting again, and the hair on his back had risen.

"Timber, come," she called.

He didn't move, waiting for her. But she hadn't given him a scent to track.

Cautiously, she made her way to her dog. The tree lay on its side, roots exposed and clinging like a giant bird's claw to a large circle of dirt that had followed its upheaval.

"Is it an animal?" she asked Timber.

Maybe she should get Cody before stepping any further, but it would be silly to call him over for nothing.

Actually, she thought, staring at what Timber had uncovered, *maybe it isn't so silly*. Rachel felt faint at the image in front of her, an image that wouldn't quite register.

There, on the ground, was a set of skeletal human remains.

Her knees buckled, taking her down to the cold snow. For a long moment, she couldn't catch her breath, couldn't swallow, couldn't look away from the bones.

As her mind slowly began to function properly again, Rachel realized last night's storm had uprooted more than the tree. It had uncovered a potentially deadly secret.

14

*H*ands gripped Rachel by the shoulders, lifted her up, and pulled her back. Thinking she was being attacked again, she whirled around with a shriek. Before she had time to form another thought, she was enveloped in a pair of strong arms.

"It's okay." Cody had her, his warm breath next to her ear.

She let out a puff of air, still feeling a bit numb, but not from the cold. Pulling away, frost stung her cheeks, reminding her that she was still alive—while someone else was not. Rachel couldn't tear her eyes from the hollowed-out earth where the skeleton lay amid a dusting of snow-laden jeans, a light-brown jacket, and hiking boots, the items ravaged by time and weather.

Cody took his phone out and tapped in a number. "Hey, Chief, you'll want to get to Nettie's place fast. We've found human remains in a hollow under a toppled tree out back."

He winced and held the phone away from his ear as a loud barrage of words echoed from it. Cody waited until the chief calmed down before he spoke again. "Yes, I'm sure they're human. Not many animals wear clothing. I'd say the remains have been here a while, but I'm not a medical examiner. No, neither of us has gone near the remains. We're standing about two feet away."

Rachel stepped back even farther. Timber stayed by her side, almost as if he wanted to keep her from getting any closer. Maybe the dog had the right idea. Rachel shivered and tore her gaze away.

Cody disconnected his call and walked her to her grandma's cabin.

"Do you think it's George Henderson?" she whispered.

"I don't know. And I don't know if this area was part of the search perimeter that went out after him, but then I wasn't here when he disappeared."

"It's hard to not think that the bones could belong to George."

Cody went out to the Jeep, came back with a couple of bottled waters, and passed one to her. Then he sat down at the kitchen table and took out his tablet.

She watched him for a moment as his fingers flew over the screen, before sitting across from him and asking, "What are you doing?"

"Reviewing George's information. Are you okay?"

She scooted her chair around the kitchen table so she could read his screen too. "I will be, but I'd have been happier to find the earring instead."

Cody shook his head. "Every turn of this trip home has brought some new surprise. One thing is pretty clear, though. I don't think that whatever happened to that person was an accident."

"The skeleton was buried too deep for the person to have simply died there," Rachel agreed. "Somebody dug a hole deep enough to discourage animals, then buried the body."

"I think so too," Cody agreed. "Wish we knew when and how your grandmother wound up with the Ankar necklace and earrings. I know we can't assume the skeleton belongs to George, but if it does, I can't help but wonder if he saw something he shouldn't have and paid a terrible price for it."

"Grandma Nettie wouldn't have been involved in anything underhanded. But tell me more about Hammonds," she urged.

Cody frowned again. "What makes you ask about Hammonds?"

"You're here hunting for a jewel thief. We have jewels popping up right and left. Add the attacks, and now a body. I'm just wondering if there is a connection. Can you describe Hammonds?"

"We don't have a specific description. He's that good. He mostly hits homes where he's formed some connection with the owners. Every surveillance video has been corrupted, missing, or destroyed. He knew where the cameras were and how to avoid them or take them out. Our best visuals came from an airport heist, where Hammonds was seen in the crowd. We know he's male, tall, and fairly thin."

"That's not super detailed, is it?"

"We think he's dark-haired, and we believe he has one buyer, probably overseas, for the jewels."

"How does he decide on a mark?"

"We don't know. He's hit both coasts as well as the Midwest. Only California has been hit more than once."

"What about Colorado?"

"That's the kicker. We've had a second anonymous tip since I arrived. Both insist that Hammonds is in the area, yet Colorado has never been a target for him. We've had no reports of stolen jewels, which is why I want to know more about the Ankar pieces."

"Any guess who provided the anonymous tips?"

Cody sat down at the table. "No, but we think they were both women. We've investigated other jewelry thieves and can't find a connection. We've called previous victims, but that hasn't been any help."

"Where did the calls come from?"

"The first was an email from a library in central Denver. We tracked down the computer, but the person it was signed out to had gotten up to use the bathroom and someone else slipped into their spot. We talked to the user who'd stepped away, and he remembers seeing a woman leaving, but she was bundled up and he couldn't describe her."

"So it could have been someone from here?" Rachel surmised.

"It's not that much of a drive."

"We are investigating that possibility, even more since you found the Ankar jewelry."

"And the second tip?"

"Burner phone."

They sat quietly for a few moments. Then Rachel asked, "Any news on Lydia Lambert?"

"Not much. By the time I got the marshals on her, she'd returned the rental car in Aspen, and a clerk said she'd walked down the street. He figured she lived in the neighborhood or was catching a bus. We're checking video cameras in the proximity. She used the same phony name but paid with a credit card this time."

"I wonder if that's why she was so upset about having her purse stolen. Maybe it was loaded with false IDs."

"You've got a vivid imagination," Cody said. "We know she was in Rolling Pine trying to find a woman, as well as a necklace—"

"See," Rachel stated. "She's involved in the jewelry hunt too."

"We know she had her purse stolen," Cody continued. "Or at least she claims she did."

"Something may have scared her," Rachel determined. "Anything else I should know?"

"One more thing about Hammonds, which I hate to tell you. After more than a decade of successful heists with no violence, his MO changed two years ago in Dallas when he robbed a family named Chapman. The family consisted of a mother, father, and two kids."

"They all died?"

Cody's voice softened. "No, just the mother and one of the kids. We think they walked in on the thief during the burglary. They'd been at a birthday party, and she realized she'd forgotten the gift at home. She went back to get it, and her son asked to go with her."

Rachel would have done the same. It was easy to picture herself in the poor woman's shoes.

"All I can say," Cody added, "is that they didn't suffer. Hammonds is as thorough a killer as he is a jewel thief. It was fast and likely painless."

"Except for her husband and other child," Rachel said. "It wasn't painless for them."

"You're right," Cody agreed. "They're still suffering, and probably always will."

Rachel gazed out the back window at the white snow. "Like George's family."

"Like George's family," Cody agreed. He stood and took a step toward the window.

Rachel joined him, watching as Chief Becker and another man stepped out of a law enforcement vehicle into the snow. Becker opened the cabin door, stuck his head in, and said, "Lead the way."

Timber went first, bursting out of the cabin and arrowing toward the overturned tree.

"Cody, Rachel, this is Devon Delaney, our medical examiner," the chief said as they followed Timber.

Devon shook Cody's hand, then Rachel's. "I retired five years ago and moved here. Every now and then a case pops up, and I get called."

Rachel didn't think the timing was right to say, "Nice to meet you," so she settled for, "I'm glad you're here."

Cody filled the team in on everything he'd noted.

They arrived at the scene. Timber edged too close, and Rachel called him back.

"I like a well-trained dog." Devon frowned at the skeletal remains, then the hollow and the surrounding area.

"He's search and rescue," Rachel explained.

"Not much to rescue here." Devon pulled a camera from a duffel bag and started taking pictures of the remains and the area.

While Chief Becker cordoned off the spot, Devon carefully maneuvered in the snow, circling the remains as he continued his photography. Occasionally Devon bent down and used a pencil from his coat pocket to rearrange a piece of the clothing for a closer shot.

Rachel was intrigued by not only the number of photos, but what was deemed relevant.

Devon seemed especially interested in the tree roots. "Any trace evidence is going to be here. It's too late to figure the escape path of whoever dug this grave."

Someone coughed. Rachel spun and noticed a few neighbors gathering to watch from a distance in Grandma Nettie's backyard. The lure of a police vehicle and something unusual happening had acted as a beacon.

Devon moved a rock from beside the skull and leaned in to take another photo. He carefully rotated the skull until it was facing left instead of right. "I'd say homicide. Bullet wound, small caliber. Our victim probably died instantly as whoever pulled the trigger knew exactly where to aim."

"How long has the body been here?" Becker asked.

"At a rough estimate, four to six years. I'll know more after I speak with a forensic pathologist."

Chief Becker pulled out his notepad. "Rachel, what time did you find the skeleton, and where was Cody?"

"It was about ten minutes after one, possibly a quarter after."

"I was here less than a minute later. I'd finished shoveling the front walk," Cody said. "I was coming to see what Rachel was doing."

"She was searching for the earring, right?"

"I was," Rachel confirmed.

"Had you been back here before?"

"No, the necklace had blown toward the front yard, so we were focusing there," Rachel said. "It could be George, couldn't it?"

Devon straightened. "Based on the size of the skull and shape of the pelvis, I'm thinking it's probably not a George. This skeleton belonged to a female."

At first, Cody thought it was Rachel screaming. But that made no sense. She hadn't screamed when she stumbled across the body. He scanned the perimeter for the source of the sound.

By his best guess, they'd been standing there maybe thirty minutes, but already a good ten or more onlookers stood shivering in the frigid air, watching as the crime scene developed.

Cody caught sight of Kristin exiting a vehicle and suddenly understood who was screaming.

Rachel saw her too and hurried across the snow, catching Kristin before she could make it to the hollow.

"Is it George? It's not George, right?" Kristin stammered.

Rachel wrapped her arms around Kristin and led her toward Nettie's house. Cody didn't envy Rachel. She could assure Kristin that the remains did not belong to George, but it was a temporary blessing. In the end, George was still missing and the reality would hit Kristin anew.

Watching their retreating figures, Cody realized how strong Rachel was. He'd always recognized it, but he also saw a sense of honor and leadership that hadn't been there before.

He made his way toward the spectators who were shuffling ever nearer. "This is as close as you get, folks."

Cell phones were raised high as onlookers took video footage.

Glancing in the direction of the toppled tree, Cody was relieved that all they could see was Chief Becker writing in his notebook and the top of the medical examiner's headgear bobbing as he moved from one position to another.

"Is it Bob?" Chris Mack stepped forward, concerned. "Some of us have been looking for him."

"It's not Bob," Cody said. "We don't know who it is. You can help by standing back rather than jumping to conclusions."

Chris must not have heard or understood Cody's suggestion because he asked, "Could it be George?"

"Please, go back to your vehicles and head home."

Rachel came out of the house, hurrying their way as a blue truck slid in behind Cody's Jeep.

Paul and George's father, Adam Henderson, jumped out. He was a big man, balding, not wearing a hat or coat. He sprinted toward Cody as if he were forty years younger.

Cody pushed his way through the small crowd of gawkers to meet him. "Mr. Henderson, go on over to Nettie's house. I'll send Chief Becker as soon as he can get away."

"No, I need to see—"

"I told you it was George," Chris announced to the crowd.

Cody leaned close, so only Mr. Henderson could hear. "It is not George."

"What?"

"It's *not* George," Cody quietly repeated, putting his arm around Mr. Henderson and steering him away from the crowd.

The older man bent over, hands on his knees. Cody sank down with him, thinking the man could be having a heart attack. Mr. Henderson wheezed, "I need to call my wife."

"Please do it from inside the house," Cody said, pointing toward

Nettie's and hoping Rachel would be okay handling another of George's distraught loved ones.

When Mr. Henderson began to trudge in that direction, Cody bypassed the gawkers and their questions and rejoined Chief Becker, asking, "Found anything new?"

"Delaney is filling evidence bags, that's all," Chief Becker said.

A clump of snow dislodged from a nearby tree and rained down on Devon. The medical examiner shook it off.

Rachel appeared and tugged on Cody's arm. Her cheeks were pink. Snow dotted her hair. She'd left her hat and scarf somewhere. "Mr. Henderson is calling both Paul and his wife," she told him. "I reassured him that the bones do not belong to his son, but I'm not sure he's completely convinced."

"What are the odds?" Cody said. "A body that was buried in the area roughly four years ago that doesn't belong to George?"

"Are we any closer to finding out who it does belong to?" Rachel asked.

Devon gave a satisfied grunt as he held up a small blue wallet. "It was deep in the left jacket pocket." Carefully, with gloved fingers, he opened it. "Belongs to an Angela Welky from Elkhorn, Nebraska. That is, if we can assume this wallet belongs with the remains."

"I know that name," Cody said.

Chief Becker raised an eyebrow. "Me too. After I went back to the office, I located my notes from when Lydia Lambert brought that photo of a missing woman into the station. Angela Welky is the woman from that photo—the woman Lydia Lambert was searching for."

"There is an Angela connected to the Ankar jewelry," Cody said. "She was related to Donald Allen, who commissioned the sets for his nieces. I wonder if Lydia Lambert is connected as well. We already know she's pretending to be someone she's not."

"Well, she's not Richard Hammonds," Rachel said.

"No, I don't believe so," Chief Becker said.

Devon poked his head out of the hollow and asked, "Richard Hammonds the jewel thief?"

"Where did you hear that name?" Cody asked.

"On a true-crime show I watch, mostly featuring stories about master thieves who have never been caught."

Before Cody could respond, Rachel's cell rang. She pulled it out, checked the screen, and answered, "Hi, Emily."

Devon was back to scavenging for clues. Becker was walking toward Nettie's cabin, no doubt to talk with Mr. Henderson and Kristin. Rachel turned her back to Cody, but he could still hear every word of her phone call with her sister.

"I completely forgot about my nail appointment. I'm so sorry. Really, I can paint my own nails. I do it all the time. I'm sorry you're upset, but . . . What's happening over there?"

Rachel shot a concerned look in Cody's direction and continued talking to Emily. "I can't get back to help out right this second. Yes, I know you have a million things to do. What? I'm sure Kristin didn't mean to be rude. Hold on a minute."

Rachel pressed the phone against her chest and said, "Apparently Kristin got a call and then rushed out of the lodge without answering questions or explaining. Justin chased after her. She shouted at him to leave her alone and tore out of the parking lot."

Cody peered toward the road. "Tell Emily that Kristin is here and Justin has arrived. Let her know we've found a body and that it does not belong to George. Emily will find out anyway. Better she hears it from you."

Rachel put the phone up to her ear once more and listened for a moment. Finally, she said, "I'm at Grandma Nettie's. Kristin and Justin are both here."

"Well, what do you know?" Devon exclaimed, no longer in the hollow. Crouching close to the root of the tree, he admired a small object dangling from the end of his pencil.

It sparkled.

Cody's mouth opened, but Rachel grasped the situation first and told her sister, "I think we've found the other earring."

*W*hen Cody determined that he'd get nothing else from the crime scene, he escorted Rachel to his parents' house, unwilling to let her out of his sight.

Rachel walked by his side in silence. He could only imagine what was going through her mind. So much whirled through his own mind that he could barely harness it. One question kept rising to the top. Was Angela Welky the granddaughter of Rayna Allen?

Rachel interrupted his thoughts. "Do you think the earring landed by the tree after the explosion or did Angela Welky bury it?"

"If the earring was buried with Welky, then it was buried around four years ago. Everything keeps circling back to that date. But if the earring landed there after the water heater explosion, then we have yet another mystery on our hands."

Before they made it to the front door, his mother had it open. "I've been so worried." She handed Rachel a towel and waited patiently while they shed their outerwear and Rachel rubbed down Timber.

"Anything you can share? Is it anyone I know?" Her voice broke.

Rachel opened her mouth, but Cody quickly took over. "Not quite yet, Mom."

"Somebody in town said you found more missing jewelry."

The lookie-loos' footage, thought Cody, remembering Devon holding up his pencil near the tree roots. He'd been filmed. No doubt Rachel had too.

"Mom, as soon as I can share more, I will. Right now, I need to check something out downstairs."

"Can I feed Timber and give him some water?" Rachel asked.

Cody opened the door to the basement and took a few steps down the stairs, pausing to hear them talk.

His mother said, "I'll cook up some hamburger meat for your dog."

"That would be perfect."

"So much excitement at your grandmother Nettie's," he heard Rose say as she opened the fridge.

"Yes," Rachel agreed.

Cody smiled. His mother wouldn't get much else from Rachel. Then Rose changed the subject, enough so that Cody climbed up one stair in order to hear better.

"You and Cody have been spending a lot of time together. How long are you staying?"

"I'm leaving the day after the wedding." Even as Rachel said the words, Cody hoped they weren't true. She was still in danger, and that danger might follow her back to Arizona. She'd stumbled onto a fortune's worth of jewels, and her family needed to make some decisions about them.

A cell phone burst out a ringtone. "That's one of the neighbors," his mother said. "She and I have been calling each other every five minutes to ask about updates. Give me just a minute."

Cody hurried down the stairs, knowing exactly what Rachel would do with his mother distracted. Sure enough, the basement door opened further and stocking feet appeared. Rachel held onto the banister and slowly made her way down the steps.

"Your lair," she commented. "It's been a while since I was down here." Her gaze passed over the pool table holding a stack of folded towels and onto a dart game nailed to the wall. Her eyes settled on the red couch that Cody had picked out, much to his mother's annoyance.

"I'm surprised she didn't get rid of it," Rachel remarked.

He loved that couch. He remembered a dozen kids down there laughing, roughhousing, playing games.

Rachel interrupted his reflection by walking over to study the photos on his corkboard.

She sucked in a breath at the section about George Henderson. Next, she studied enlarged photos of the necklace, earring, and bracelet—her discoveries. They only briefly held her interest.

"Who's this?" She pointed to an older gentleman dressed circa 1960.

"Donald Allen. He's the man who commissioned the Ankar jewelry sets and gave them to his nieces." Cody touched each photo of the five young women flanking Donald's.

Rachel leaned forward and read aloud the names of each niece, noting the dates underneath. She put out a finger to trace the lineage Cody had marked under each one and stopped on Rayna.

"Yes," Cody said quietly. "Angela Welky owned a set of Ankar jewelry. I'm thinking someone killed her to get it."

Rachel leaned toward a photo of Angela as a small girl sitting astride an elephant with her sister and grandmother. "It's so sad that this sweet, happy girl has been reduced to what we found outside. Did she live around here?"

"I don't think so."

"I'll call Kristin and ask her if she knows anything about—no, she's dealing with enough. I'll call my mother."

"Becker will handle all of that. He wouldn't appreciate us getting there first. You and I, however, should take a trip."

"Where? And why do I need to go?"

Cody tapped one of the larger photos of the five nieces together. "We're going to Nebraska to find Betty, the middle niece, age ninety-eight. She's still alive. And I want you along so that I can keep you safe."

"We need to let her know we're coming," Rachel said.

"I agree. We'll call on the way. While you were in Nettie's with Kristin and Mr. Henderson, I called my office. They've already started putting the trip together." Cody checked his watch. "If we leave now, we can be in Omaha by six or seven at the latest."

"I need to take Timber back to the lodge."

"My mom will look after him. She loves dogs. We need to get to the family before Welky's name makes it to the news stations. Time is not on our side." He gently nudged her toward the stairs. "Please go up and ask my mother to prepare a few sandwiches. I need to make some phone calls, and then we'll be good to go."

In less than twenty minutes, they were in his Jeep, heading to Aspen where they'd board a small plane to Denver, and switch to a jet for the rest of the trip.

Cody couldn't drive nearly as fast as he wanted to. The roads were icy, with low visibility.

Next to him, Rachel called her sister. Similar to their last phone conversation, when Emily informed Rachel she'd missed her nail appointment, Rachel did a lot of listening and not much talking. It sounded as if Emily wasn't too surprised Rachel had decided to ride along with Cody to Denver to fetch something he'd forgotten.

Disconnecting the call, Rachel said, "She's worried that we won't be back in time for the rehearsal."

Something in her tone made him glance from the road to her face. "What else?"

Rachel shook her head.

"I'm going to bug you from here to Nebraska if you don't tell me. I've been trained to extract information."

Rachel sighed. "She ended the call by saying, 'It's not like you were here for me during my last wedding.'"

He wanted to reach over, take her hand, and say something that would undo her hurt, but nothing he could tell Rachel would change what happened between the sisters, or what was still happening.

Rachel stared out the window at the black ice below and the gray sky above. Last night's storm was evidenced by the piles of snow on the sides of the highway. The cold wind pressed against the windows, but Cody's heater worked against it, and somehow just simply being with him added a certain kind of warmth.

She took out the sandwiches and bottled water his mother had packed, and they ate companionably. Every once in a while, Cody spoke hands-free on his phone using the speaker, getting updates on what was happening in Rolling Pine. In one call, they learned that the skeletal remains they'd found had been moved to the morgue. Rachel found herself grateful, in a bittersweet sort of way, that Angela Welky was finally beginning the process of being properly laid to rest.

When the call finally ended, Cody told Rachel, "There is very little information available on Lydia Lambert, which is why I think she might be connected to Richard Hammonds. They're both ghosts who apparently don't exist and who are practiced in the art of disappearing."

"And you think Richard Hammonds is still in Rolling Pine?"

"I do," he said. "And I wish I'd had time to visit more of the town's new residents. The ones I did check out all seem aboveboard."

Rachel rested her cheek against the cool glass window, thinking of her family. They were all shocked about the remains found on Nettie's land, but they had no idea the depth of what was going on—the real danger or how it might affect them.

The shimmering lights of Aspen beckoned on the horizon. When Cody pulled into the small airport's parking lot, a man jogged over to meet them. A moment later, Cody helped Rachel from the vehicle, and they boarded a small private plane.

During the short flight, Cody read the contents of a yellow folder. He made notes and checked information on his tablet. Rachel passed the time talking to Jake, the pilot, about his dog—a malamute who liked to eat socks, aptly named Socks.

The minute they landed, two men headed their way. One helped Rachel out of the little plane and ushered her down a wet, slick runway onto the steps of a much bigger plane, and then to two seats in the back.

Everyone on the plane gaped at them as they got settled.

Rachel leaned toward the agent and whispered, "Did they hold this plane for us?"

"Yes, and they offered two people money to give up these seats and take a later flight."

Cody boarded a few minutes later and sat beside her, carrying a new set of blue folders.

The flight attendant reminded everyone that she'd gone over safety procedures already and told them to "enjoy the trip."

When the other travelers' attention was no longer on them, Rachel whispered to Cody, "What's in the folders?"

"A history of the Allen family."

"Anyone we should pay special attention to?"

"So far, I continue to be awed by Rayna, the youngest niece."

"The one on the elephant?"

"Yes. Her granddaughters are equally fascinating. Sheila is a doctor in her fifties, who moves from one third world country to another, doing as much good as she can. We've got two photos of her from articles she's published. She has two children in college, both on their way to becoming doctors as well."

"No social media?"

"Limited for the entire family, as if they feel no need for it."

Sometimes Rachel felt the same way, but social media was necessary to advertise her business. "What did Angela do?"

"She was a few years younger than Sheila and an amateur archeologist, which might explain why she was dressed in such a way that we assumed she was George. According to what we could find, she traveled a lot and disappeared frequently. Her family reported her missing twice. Both times she turned up in some obscure place."

"Does Sheila know Angela is dead?"

"In truth, we can't be certain that Angela is dead. So far, our only proof is the identification from her wallet, which could have been placed there by someone else. Still, once we have positive identification, we know that Sheila is currently working in a remote region of Haiti, so we'll be able to get in touch with her."

"How do you know this so quickly?"

"Because of my work on the Richard Hammonds case. With all of the jewelry found in Rolling Pine that links to the Allen family, the US Marshals are fully invested in finding the connection to our jewel thief."

"What else did you find out about Angela Welky?"

Cody pulled two photos from a folder. "These are from a thirty-year-old college yearbook. Here's the thing—four years ago, Angela married a younger man named Stephen Bale."

"Around when George disappeared?" Rachel asked.

"Exactly. Here's where it gets tricky. Like Lydia Lambert, we can't find proof that Stephen Bale exists. The information he provided for the marriage certificate and driver's license is false."

They sifted through information about the Allen family from the folders.

"We might be in luck," Rachel said after reading a newspaper article regarding Betty Manchester, Donald Allen's middle niece. "Betty is one of the oldest living graduates of her alma mater."

Cody nodded, more interested in what little they had about Angela Bale, nee Welky. "Angela didn't even have time to change the name on her driver's license. If the remains belong to her, then she must have been killed on her honeymoon or shortly thereafter."

They landed in Omaha a little before midnight. A slim man met them at the airport and handed over keys to a small dark sedan, which contained a full tank of gas and two cold waters.

Omaha was much bigger than Rolling Pine, and Elkhorn turned out to be a good distance from the city. Rachel passed the journey staring out the dark car window, wondering what lay ahead.

When they finally saw a sign indicating that Elkhorn was five miles away, Rachel was very nearly drifting off to sleep. Trying to stay awake, she finished her bottled water and stretched her upper body as best she could in the confines of the car.

Elkhorn Manor Retirement Home sat atop a short hill with a curving driveway, surrounded by trees, benches, and snow. A few lights were on inside the building. Visitor parking, empty except for one vehicle, was located to the left of a huge front porch. Cody pulled into a spot and then came around to open the door for Rachel.

The front doors were locked, so Cody rang a bell. A security guard arrived and Cody held up his badge. Together he and Rachel entered a deserted foyer. A small room to the right held a grand piano. To the left was a reception area. A woman waited in the foyer, wearing a somber expression.

Cody approached her, hand outstretched. "Mrs. Bush, thank you for meeting us."

Tina Bush, a tall, thin redhead who appeared to be in her fifties, shook his hand. "I can't say I was surprised by your call. When I told Mom this might have to do with Cousin Angela, she was adamant about seeing you. I suggested we do this tomorrow morning, but she said she wouldn't be able to sleep until she spoke with you. Not that she sleeps much anyway."

Tina spoke to a security guard, who buzzed open a door. She led the visitors to an elevator, and they rode up to the second floor, exiting into a hallway. Each door bore a resident's name engraved on a brass marker. Betty Manchester's room was halfway down the corridor, her door already open.

"Hi, Mom," Tina called out, entering and closing the door behind them. Cody and Rachel followed Tina through a tiny kitchen into a living room large enough for a couch, an easy chair, a bookcase, and a television. A door to one side probably led to a bedroom. Every inch of the walls was covered with framed family photos.

Betty Manchester was a tiny woman tucked into the easy chair, her short hair perfectly white. Pink pajama pants peeked out from under a robe sporting a pocket embroidered with Betty's name. She picked up a glass of water from a small table, her hand shaking a little. She took a sip before speaking. "Must be pretty important for such a last-minute visit."

Betty waved an arm for them to sit, and Cody and Rachel perched on the couch.

Betty leaned forward. "How did Angela die, and how long ago?"

"First, I have to remind you that we do not yet have a positive ID, but I feel it's safe to assume that the remains we found belong to Angela Welky. The medical examiner estimates that they have been there approximately four years." Cody's voice faltered, as if he suddenly realized he was breaking traumatic news to a woman who was nearly a hundred years old.

"Please go on," Betty said. "I have experienced the deaths of many loved ones."

Cody's face contorted, but Rachel had to admire how quickly he regrouped. "The person, who we may assume was Angela Welky, was shot."

A noise came from near the doorway, and Betty called out, "You might as well join us."

The door opened, and Lydia Lambert stepped into the room.

16

*C*ody addressed the woman standing in the doorway. "Hello, Ms. Lambert. Or should I call you something else?"

"My real name is Monica Benjamin."

"My sister," Tina explained.

"You've visited Rolling Pine often," Cody said.

"Whenever I could get away from work," Monica admitted. "I was looking for my cousin Angela but didn't report her missing because I didn't think anyone would believe me. See, Angela was a free spirit. It wasn't the first time she'd gone off the grid. I had already reported her missing five times. She always appeared again after a while, and the police told me it was futile for me to keep thinking she'd disappeared when she had a pattern of going off on her own."

"Most of us didn't worry the last time she disappeared," Tina said. "But Monica was sure things were different this time."

"Good thing," Cody said.

Monica sat down. "When did you first begin to suspect that I wasn't who I pretended to be?"

"When your purse went missing."

Monica nodded. "That terrified me. My real name was in that purse. If the wrong person found it, everything would be ruined."

"Did you ever end up finding it?"

"No, and after someone used my credit card to purchase a metal detector, I hightailed it back here and came to stay with Grandma."

Cody waited for her to continue. He'd found the method effective in other interviews.

"The first time I saw you," Monica said, "I knew you were some type of law enforcement. I figured that you were working on a case, but I couldn't sort out why you were involved with the lodge owner's daughter's wedding." She peered at him. "Jewelry, right? Your assignment has to do with jewelry. Or did that become a side investigation?"

"Not a side investigation, but I am hunting for a jewelry thief." Cody studied the woman in front of him, noting her pressed pants, tucked-in blouse, and brown boots. She was still nicely dressed, but drastically different from the overdressed Lydia Lambert. "You wouldn't happen to know anything about the jewelry Rachel keeps finding, would you?"

"I never got to see it."

Cody brought out his phone, opened his photos, and passed it to Monica. Her eyes filled immediately. She passed the phone to Tina and Betty.

Betty gasped. "Those are our Ankars."

"Which of these photos are of Angela?" Rachel asked, gesturing to the photos on the wall.

Monica pointed to one above the television. "Five years ago. She was doing a pilgrimage walk in Spain."

"We thought Monica was losing her mind when she started searching for Angela this time," Tina said. "Angela vanished so often. Plus, she was newly married at the time, to quite a wealthy young man. We all assumed she and her new husband were out exploring, having the time of their lives."

Monica wiped away a tear. "I wanted to believe that, but my cousin and I were close, and Angela would have brought her husband home to meet me. It didn't make sense to me that she hadn't."

"I thought perhaps she was embarrassed," Betty said. "She was almost fifteen years older than the man she married."

"That's nothing to be embarrassed about. People marry younger spouses all the time," Monica added. "In case my fears were unfounded, I allowed some time to pass before I decided to try to find her."

"Two years ago, Monica came home from a trip to Rolling Pine with Angela's favorite watch, which had been a gift from her husband," Betty said.

Monica disappeared into Betty's bedroom and came back carrying an envelope, a jewelry box, and what appeared to be an ordinary watch. But Cody doubted anything was ordinary with these ladies.

Monica set down the other items and spread the watch across her palm. "This is a very rare upscale piece, with yellow gold, diamonds, and mother-of-pearl." She handed the watch to Cody.

Cody took the piece and turned it over in his hand.

"I'd been rambling around Rolling Pine, randomly showing Angela's photo to anyone who would give me the time of day, but no one recognized her. Then one day I was in the library and I watched the librarian take off this very watch, pass it around to a bunch of small children during story time, and lay it on a shelf. I took a good look at it and almost passed out."

"So you stole it."

Monica frowned. "I wouldn't put it that way. After all, I'm certain it belonged to Angela. She loved it, so I don't think she would have given it away."

"Why didn't you tell the police?"

"Because I needed to find real proof that something had happened to my cousin aside from finding her watch by accident."

"Did you know that the librarian had received the watch as a gift from Bob Lewis?"

"Yes. I read the police report after the librarian reported it stolen. She must have done some research and found out what it was worth." Monica opened the jewelry box. "Bob came up again, with more of Angela's jewelry." She handed Cody a set of earrings. "These belonged to my cousin, and they're worth about thirty-five thousand dollars. Your friend Paul had them priced at seven."

Cody took the small oblong earrings.

"I purchased them from Paul's consignment display on my most recent visit. He said Bob had brought them in."

"Why didn't you go to Chief Becker?" Rachel asked. "Surely you had enough evidence that something strange was going on, so don't you think he'd listen?"

"Believe me, I wanted to. But someone had attacked you, Miss Andrews. My going to the police might put not just me, but also my family in danger. I was ready to leave Rolling Pine the day somebody stole my purse."

"Bob would never—"

"I don't think he had anything to do with Angela's disappearance, or her death," Monica assured her. "But I do think he knows where the rest of Angela's jewelry is. At least some of it."

"Maybe she gave it to him," Betty said.

"Why would she do that?" Rachel asked.

"Angela had been to Rolling Pine before. Maybe she thought Bob was someone she could trust," Betty responded.

"But why would she need to trust anyone with her jewelry, and why would she have taken the Ankar pieces with her?" Monica said.

"Have you tried speaking to Bob?" Cody asked.

"I have," Lydia said. "But he acted like he didn't know what I was talking about. I've searched his place—both the mobile home and old cabin—but I didn't find the jewelry. And if he has been selling off

Angela's jewels for some reason, he's clearly not using it to improve his station in life."

"He doesn't care about money," Rachel said.

"Angela didn't either. Of course, it's easy to not care about money when you have plenty of it. As I said, Angela was a free spirit, and it wouldn't have surprised me to find out that she gave away expensive belongings on a whim."

Cody leaned forward. "So you think that Angela gave her jewels to Bob?"

"If she did, maybe my cousin thought she was helping Bob, or perhaps she gave them to him for safekeeping for some reason, and it's possible Bob's forgotten that."

Cody checked his phone, but he'd received nothing from Becker to let him know whether or not Bob had been found. Quickly, he sent a text asking for an update. There were other things to figure out too.

"What I can't trace," Cody said, "is the Ankar bracelet that Rachel found."

"Oh, that," Betty said, rolling her eyes. "Rayna was Uncle Donald's favorite. A year after he gave us all the Ankar sets, he commissioned the bracelet for Rayna's birthday, which caused quite a stir among my sisters. He didn't make that mistake again. He died not long after that, or I'm sure we would all have matching bracelets. He did love and dote on all of us."

Monica said, "Bob probably has, or had, some of the jewelry, but not all of it. I'm obviously not the only one searching for the pieces, and I think the same thing you do. Rachel keeps finding the jewelry, and whoever is after it besides me still wants it, which keeps her in danger."

"Do you have any leads?" Cody asked. "I'm grateful for any information you can give me. We've been stuck on this, and you've already filled in several pieces we were missing."

Monica ducked her head. "I wanted to loop you in. I don't know why, but I feel I can trust you. If you hadn't shown up tonight, I would have called you with this detail in the morning. I assume you know that Stephen Bale—at least the one Angela thought she married—doesn't exist."

"We had pieced that together," Cody said.

"I hired a private investigator two months ago. That's when I discovered the fabrication. You have no idea how good it feels to have someone to tell this to, someone to believe me." Monica held up the envelope. "The private detective tracked down a clerk who served as one of the witnesses when Angela and Stephen married. They'd told the clerk they didn't want any photos taken, but she took one when they weren't paying attention, in case they changed their minds later."

Cody found himself hanging on Monica's every word.

"The PI sent me an email with an attachment. The picture was blurry and I don't like leaving a trail, so I flew home. One of my daughters is talented at photo restoration and enhancement, so she came over to see if we could get a cleaner copy." She held out an envelope. "It's not the clearest shot of the newlyweds, but it was enough to make me believe that the man Angela married was actually Richard Hammonds. Though I'm not certain yet."

"How did you come to this conclusion?" Cody asked. "Where did you even hear about Richard Hammonds."

"I researched jewelry thieves. Then, when you found the Ankar necklace, I knew I wasn't crying wolf, so I contacted the authorities."

"You were one of the anonymous tips," Cody guessed.

"You mean there was more than one?" Monica sat up straighter. "Good."

Opening the envelope, Cody said, "Yes, we had another tip come in at Thanksgiving."

"I've emailed Chief Becker a copy of this photo," Monica said. "I'm hoping it'll help him identify Hammonds."

Cody pulled a photo from the envelope. Rachel peered over his shoulder at a picture showing a long wooden counter lined with computers. The walls were textured brown, adorned with an American flag and an oversize clock. Underneath the clock stood a tall woman in a bright-red dress, smiling down at her left hand. Angela Welky.

But standing next to her—

Rachel covered her mouth in shock.

Next to Angela stood a tall, lanky man with short brown hair and high cheekbones.

Rachel grabbed Cody's hand as her gaze shot up to meet his.

The man standing next to Angela was none other than Stephen Bale. Alias Richard Hammonds.

Also known to Cody and Rachel as Justin Fletcher.

"Can't we fly any faster?" Rachel appreciated Monica's speed in calling the family's pilot, arranging for their private jet to be readied, and getting Rachel and Cody on board the aircraft for their trip back to Aspen.

But after some delay, she was sure the flight would be the longest of her life.

Neither Monica nor Cody answered. Monica's eyes were closed, and her head was bowed in silence. Her face was pale, as it had been since Rachel told her that in a matter of days, Rachel's sister was set to marry the man who'd likely killed Angela.

Cody was tapping rapidly on his phone, likely compiling everything they'd learned. He'd called the Marshals before they'd taken off, and a team was heading to Rolling Pine. His talk with Chief Becker had the local law enforcement bound for Rocky Mountains Lodge.

Leaning back, Rachel closed her eyes. Over and over, she replayed her conversation with Emily, who had been understandably angry and confused when Rachel had called, hoping to warn her sister before everything came out in the open.

"Justin's not here!" Emily had screeched. "I haven't seen him since late morning, and he's not answering his phone. He's blocked the app I use to locate him."

"I'm leaving Nebraska, and—"

"Nebraska? This isn't funny, Rachel. Hold on. A bunch of police officers just walked through our front door. Hello, can I help you? Did something happen to Justin?"

Emily had paused for a moment during the call. Then Chief Becker came on the line. "I've got the whole family here, Rachel. Your dad already knows about Justin—or rather Hammonds. Dennis is telling Emily as we speak."

A loud wail was followed by the phone disconnecting.

Tears dried on Rachel's cheeks, her throat still tight following that terrible phone call. *Poor Emily.*

Monica must have seen her distress, because she reached across the aisle to rest a hand on Rachel's arm. "We'll get him, Rachel. He doesn't get to destroy both our families."

"It could have been much worse. She could have gone through with marrying Justin," Cody said, his voice rough as he came to sit beside Rachel and pulled her into his arms. "He could have killed you."

It felt good to be in his arms, to have him beside her giving her strength until they landed in Aspen. She didn't know how else to cope with the dreadful hollow feeling in her chest.

They exited the plane and ran to Cody's Jeep. Cody stayed on the phone over speaker as the miles swept by, comforting her when he could. "Your family is safe, Rachel. But they still haven't found Bob yet."

When Cody and Rachel finally arrived in Rolling Pine, the sun was emerging over a gray, snow-covered early morning. All Rachel wanted was to get home, hug Emily, and make sure everyone—including Bob—was safe.

When they pulled into the Rocky Mountains Lodge parking lot, her dad, mom, and Emily all came running down the front steps.

Rachel burst from the car and dashed to meet them. For a brief moment, she forgot the fear and the drama, simply reveling in the cocoon of her family.

"The search will start at daylight," Dennis said. "Most people believe Justin's long gone by now."

Rachel didn't believe it. "He still wants the jewelry."

"It's not worth sticking around for," Emily said. "The whole town knows what he's done—possibly killing Angela Welky, trying to hurt you, and who knows what else?"

Rachel reached out and took Emily's hand. "Especially hurting you." Emily's lower lip trembled.

Her mother gathered both girls close. "We've got a buffet set up in the breakfast room. You and Cody must be hungry."

Suddenly, Rachel was hungry. Glancing over her shoulder to check on Cody's whereabouts, she found him deep in conversation with two law enforcement officers. Cody noticed her and held up a finger to let her know he'd be along momentarily.

"Where's Kristin?" Rachel asked.

"Right behind you." Kristin came up alongside Emily, reaching out to take her hand.

In the tiny restaurant, groups of police officers sat at tables, maps spread in front of them as they planned their search for Hammonds.

Rachel's dad sat down beside her, patted her arm, and tried to reassure her. "It will be all right."

Her mother fetched a plate of food. The smell of eggs and sausage was tempting, but Rachel found she couldn't eat.

Emily and Kristin each sat down with a plate.

"We were so worried," Emily told Rachel. "I mean, I knew you were safe with Cody, but when Chief Becker came by and we heard the extent of what was going on, I was so afraid. I just can't believe all of this."

Rachel picked up her fork and stabbed a tiny piece of egg. If she pretended to eat, maybe she'd have time to figure out what to say.

Emily pushed her plate away, untouched. "Justin's room is empty. It's as if he never existed. I don't even know when he cleared out his stuff. It could have been yesterday morning. It could have been last week or today. How could I not have known something was going on with my own fiancé?" Emily rested her head in her arms and gazed up at Rachel and Kristin. "I loved him, you know?"

Rachel understood that Emily was referring to Tyler.

"He was your boyfriend," Emily continued. "I knew I was making a huge mistake, but I couldn't help my feelings. It was the best and most awful time ever."

"It's okay. I got over it." And Rachel meant every word.

"But I didn't. You did nothing wrong, yet you were the one who left, who had to get away from everything and everyone you knew. I'm so, so sorry."

"Thank you," Rachel whispered, her eyes welling with tears.

"When you went back to college," Emily said, "I decided to find out if Tyler was interested in me. I had to know."

"It doesn't matter now," Rachel said.

"When I discovered that he was, we fell in love in a matter of days."

No one spoke. Rachel's parents looked as stricken as she felt.

"In a matter of days," Emily repeated. "I thought I would never be done grieving Tyler, so no one was more surprised than I was when I fell in love with Justin. I can't believe it was all a lie."

Silence ensued for several moments as Kristin comforted Emily and Rachel absorbed the apology she'd been waiting years to hear.

Finally, Cody joined the family. "What has Chief Becker told you all?"

"Not enough," said Rachel's dad.

Cody filled them in on everything he and Rachel had learned from their trip to Nebraska.

"So technically," Emily said, "even though Hammonds and I were to be wed on Saturday, he was already married to someone named Angela Welky, who may or may not be dead."

"Nothing would have been legal about either marriage," Cody said.

"And you say he was in town hunting for the Ankar jewels?" her mom asked.

"And a few more pieces. Apparently, Angela was known to carry her favorites with her when she traveled."

Rachel's mom leaned forward, her voice hard. "What better cover while he searched than engagement to a local girl? Thanks to Emily's circle of friends, he was welcome everywhere. Plus, since he was working for me at the real estate office, he had access to empty homes and businesses."

"So no one suspected him," Cody finished.

Kristin raised her hand. "Actually, I did, and I called the US Marshal tip line around Thanksgiving. But I never expected Cody to sweep in like James Bond."

"What made you suspicious?" Cody asked.

"A true-crime show about a known jewel thief. The episode included what little footage the authorities have of him from an airport. First, it was the way he walked. Then, there was something about his profile. But what really convinced me was two months ago when we went to Aspen to work a booth for the Fall Festival."

"He was so handsome. All dressed up," Emily remembered.

"Justin—or rather, Hammonds—wore cuff links to the festival," Kristin explained. "That's when everything dropped into place. In the airport clip, Hammonds was walking, almost out of frame, wearing a black suit jacket with a white shirt underneath, and he was tugging at a cuff link. He had a certain way about the tugging. I noticed because he's left-handed, so the way he did it was a bit awkward, but he did it often, almost like a nervous tic. Justin used the same exact motion."

Rachel felt a stab of shock and grabbed Cody's arm. "Male, white, tall, and left-handed. At least that's how he carried his gun."

"That's how you described the man running away from Nettie's the day of the explosion," he said.

"All the clues were there," Kristin said.

"Then there was the stolen purse and the purchase of a metal detector."

"Dumb luck that he stole a purse belonging to Angela Welky's sister."

"I didn't see any of this." Emily turned on Kristin. "Why didn't you tell me? Why didn't you stop this engagement from happening before it got so far? I would have listened to you."

Kristin shook her head. "I couldn't tell you until I was certain and the police had caught him. I thought you were truly happy. You were smiling again, and I didn't want to take that from you until I had to."

"But it was dangerous."

Everyone's eyes were on Kristin. She lifted her chin. "I couldn't take the chance. I had to believe that if I was right, he would be caught before anything happened to you. You lost a sister with your first marriage. If I told you what I believed about Justin, and I had been wrong, you would have lost a best friend with your second marriage."

$\mathcal{C}$ody's parents showed up as the law enforcement teams were readying to leave, bringing along Timber and homemade baked goods. Cody reflected that he might be the only US Marshal in history to have a mother send off a team with stomachs full of milk and cookies.

In the end, there were four Marshals and five local police officers. If Cody knew Rolling Pine, there'd be a few locals joining the hunt as well, which wasn't ideal, but the residents knew the Arapahoe National Forest. Plus, there was a five-thousand-dollar reward for information leading to the capture of one Richard Hammonds.

Hammonds, however, was not first on the agenda.

"Robert Lewis is approximately eighty years old. He's about five foot ten and 205 pounds," Cody told the Marshals. "He was last seen wearing dark-blue work pants, a brown down jacket, a yellow cap, black boots, and brown suede gloves."

Cody's gloves.

Every single law enforcement officer studied the photo they'd been given.

"His dog, Biggles, made his way to Shelley David's an hour ago. Biggles is slightly dehydrated, but he's being cared for at the veterinary office. Dr. Levy says he'll be fine."

There were four teams, each consisting of one Marshal and one local officer. Two teams would knock on doors and search empty buildings. Rachel's mom and dad were traveling with those teams, as the Andrewses owned much of the town and, as a real estate agent, Virginia had keys to much of the other half. A third team was assigned the forest trails and Bob's favorite spots around town. The final team, headed by Cody, was assigned to the area around Bob's homestead.

Everyone knew that searching for Bob might lead to Hammonds. After all, Hammonds wanted the jewels and Bob allegedly had them.

Rachel's mom fussed over her and Timber. "If I'd known how dangerous your profession is, I'd have forbidden you to go into it. This is absolutely terrifying."

"It's not usually this dangerous." She grimaced at Cody as her mother tugged her zipper up higher.

Cody held up his hands. "Hey, don't look at me for help. My mother's handing everyone plastic bags of chocolate chip cookies to bring along."

"I can't believe I didn't think to make anything for people to take with them," Virginia said, shrugging into her coat. "I'm so glad Rose did."

"I'm impressed with what I see, Cody." Dennis stood next to Virginia. "When you brought in that black coat from lost and found, I realized how well-organized this operation would be."

"Thank you, but your daughter deserves most of the credit for that."

When the Marshals had signed Rachel and Timber on to assist half an hour before, she and Emily had gone through Justin's room for anything they could use to scent. Not even a shred of paper, soda can in the trash, or toothpaste residue in the sink had been left behind.

Then Cody, who had spent the hours of travel poring over his notes, had remembered the black coat Rachel had discovered in the lost and found. It had been a single mention in his notes, but enough to arrange for its return to Rolling Pine in case they needed it.

"It might not work," Rachel warned as she and Cody made their way to his Jeep. Chief Becker would follow in his police vehicle.

"Let's not worry about that yet and focus on Bob first. We can get a piece of clothing from the mobile home for Timber to scent." His concern, which he wouldn't share with Rachel, was that finding Bob might mean finding another victim. Now that they knew Justin and Hammonds were one and the same, the mess at Bob's place made him think someone had tossed the place.

"Half the town has been at Bob's place trying to find him."

"Yes, but the locals didn't know about Hammonds. They'd assume, rightly so, that Bob would seek warmer temperatures to hole up in."

"To think, as far as we know, Bob disappeared the night of Emily's shower. He could be anywhere by now, and in any condition."

Cody didn't want to add his concern to Rachel's trail of thoughts. In his profession, justice often prevailed, but there was almost always a cost.

His phone buzzed, and he hit the speaker icon. "Cody Scott here."

"Oddest thing," said a colleague from the US Marshal headquarters. "You know how we put a tracker on Bob Lewis's phone yesterday?"

"The service provider could only pinpoint the phone's last location as Bob's property. And that was from a month ago," Cody said.

"Correct, but guess what? We got a call from the service provider. The phone has been powered on this morning."

"Really?"

"Yes, and here's the really strange thing. GPS is still putting it on Bob's property."

"You think Bob is back home and found his phone?" Rachel asked after Cody finished the call.

"What I think is that we need to hurry." Cody pressed down on the gas pedal, called Chief Becker to relay the news, and moments later parked on the side of the road by Bob's property. The chief pulled up shortly after.

"We were here yesterday morning," Rachel said softly. "How is that possible? It feels as if so much has happened."

"And the driveway still hasn't been touched by a shovel."

Timber leapt from the Jeep.

Cody bounded up the first step of the mobile home. But Timber took off running, away from the dilapidated cabin and back to the area he'd alerted to yesterday.

"There's something out there," Rachel said, starting after her dog. "I should have trusted him yesterday."

"What happened yesterday?" Chief Becker joined them.

"Timber alerted, but I hadn't given him a scent."

"Did he go that far yesterday?" Chief Becker asked.

"Not quite, but I called him back."

Becker took out his gun, tucked it in his jacket pocket, and joined Cody behind Rachel, who followed her dog through the damp, heavy snow until he stopped.

Timber stood perfectly still, watching them approach over his shoulder. When they got closer, the dog moved to an area in the snow where broken pieces of wood interrupted the pure expanse of pristine white powder. He pawed the area and whined.

"One of the old Lewis mine shafts," Cody said.

"With rotting wood." Chief Becker carefully tugged one of the planks. It came easily enough. Cody joined in, but when Rachel stepped forward to help, Cody stopped her. "It's a hole in the ground. One misstep and you could take a plunge."

"So could you," Rachel pointed out.

Cody kept moving the lumber. "Yes, but I'm taller and— Get back!"

Chief Becker jumped away. Unhindered by the remaining bits and pieces of wood, snow caved in, and a hole roughly four or five feet in diameter opened up. Cody pulled out a flashlight and carefully stepped to the edge. Chief Becker, a few feet away, fisted his hand in Cody's jacket, keeping him from toppling into the chasm.

Sending the flashlight beam underground, Cody waited for his eyes to adjust to the dark recess. Before they did, a weak voice echoed up the shaft.

"About time you found me," Bob said.

"About time is right," growled a voice right behind Rachel.

An arm snapped around her waist and yanked her backward. Her feet slipped out from under her. Her hat fell off, and something hard pressed against her temple.

"Don't do it, Hammonds," Cody barked.

Chief Becker went for his pocket, the butt of his gun coming into view. The hardness of the weapon that had been pressed against Rachel's temple disappeared.

Suddenly, there was an explosion of sound near Rachel's ear, as if the air had split. It was deafening at first, then followed by a tinny ringing.

Chief Becker collapsed into the hole.

Cody glanced down into the gaping maw, then glared at Hammonds. Rachel tensed as the hot muzzle of the still-smoking gun returned near her left temple.

"I'm sure you have many weapons on you," Hammonds said, "but as you can see, I'm trigger-happy, and I don't miss. There's a drop ladder in a pile to your left. You're going to toss your phone and service weapon into the snow, then climb down the ladder to join your friends."

"Why?" Cody asked.

"Because I'm pretty sure there's a fortune in jewelry down there, and you're going to find it for me. I really wanted the Ankar pieces, but the rest of Angela's jewelry is worth so much more."

"Why—?"

"Climb," Hammonds snarled. "I have a gun to your girlfriend's head. Are you really going to stand there and argue?"

Rachel wanted to say something, wanted to tell Cody to shoot Hammonds, wanted to do something, anything, to take Hammonds down. But she was frozen, not from the weather, but from pure undiluted fear.

Cody wasn't moving fast enough for Hammonds. The muzzle pressed harder, and she let out a whimper against her will.

Cody's service pistol and cell phone hit the snow a good three feet from where he stood. Rachel watched in silence as Cody found the ladder and tossed it into the hole, his green eyes holding hers until he disappeared down the mine shaft.

Hammonds finally took the gun away from Rachel's temple and pulled her toward the hole, his grip like a vise on her upper arm. The minute the ladder went slack, Hammonds pocketed his gun and pulled up the ladder. "Smart man."

Rachel glared while Hammonds took out his phone, fingers flying over the screen. Did he have an accomplice? Perhaps even one in town?

"This is your fault, you know." Hammonds put the phone away and pulled his gun back out as he stepped a few feet away from the hole, dragging Rachel with him. "You and that stupid dog. If you hadn't seen me leaving your grandmother's house, none of this would have happened."

Rachel flinched. What had Hammonds done with Timber? Normally, he would have protected her, or at least warned her that someone was sneaking up on her. "Where is my dog?"

Hammonds didn't answer, and Rachel swallowed, fighting for breath, struggling to get loose. Hammonds didn't even stumble at her effort.

She needed to keep him talking. Maybe one of the other teams would try to radio and find them. Surely, down in the mine, Cody was using Becker's cell phone if he could get a signal. "What were you doing at my Grandma Nettie's anyway?"

Her voice sounded strange, as if it came from a distance. If she weren't already about to die, she might have to worry about hearing loss from having a gun fired next to her ear.

Hammonds rolled his eyes. "Looking for jewelry, of course. I knew Bob had it. Angela talked about her friend before we came here on our honeymoon. I knew she'd become suspicious that I was hiding my real identity, but I didn't realize she'd go so far as to hide her family's most valuable treasures. And Bob was being such a fool. I didn't dare threaten him because I wasn't even sure he'd understand what was going on. So I befriended him instead, for all the good that did. I've searched this property a dozen times and finally concluded that he hid the jewelry around town—at your grandmother's, with Shelley David, even with Paul Henderson."

A faint headache started to form. Rachel used every bit of strength she had to force herself to stand up straighter. "You were marrying my sister just so you'd have more opportunities to hunt for Angela's jewelry?"

Justin snorted and called into the hole, "Found anything yet? I'm getting antsy. Especially my trigger finger."

"Not yet," came Cody's voice.

Hammonds nodded toward the hole. "Your US Marshal happens to be Emily's ex-boyfriend. What are the odds? Then he has photos of me in his basement. That's when I realized I was running out of time."

"You broke into his house?"

"I've broken into everyone's house in this town. It wasn't that difficult since I've been working with your mother's realty office. It was so easy getting into your room to drug Timber so that I could switch out the earring. As easy as it was to steal Monica's purse."

"Becker's hurt bad," Bob said. "He could be dying."

"The sooner you give up the jewels, the sooner you're out of there," Hammonds replied coldly. "More hunting and less talking. Or don't you care about saving your friends?"

"How many people are you willing to kill?" Rachel demanded.

"I didn't intend to kill anyone this time. You messed things up when you saw me running from Nettie's."

"I didn't know it was you."

"And I couldn't take a chance that you'd suddenly realize it was. Still, after the second day, when you didn't say anything, I started to relax. Maybe you genuinely didn't know, or maybe you'd decided to be smart and not say anything after I warned you off with the attack."

There was something wrong with a man whose idea of relaxing was deciding not to take someone's life.

"Were you going to kill my sister like you killed Angela?" Rachel had to ask, had to know.

Hammonds shook his head. "Believe it or not, no. See, I let myself get distracted. If I'm capable of falling in love—and I'm not totally convinced I am—well, I came pretty close with your sister."

Rachel was so frightened that she struggled to breathe, her ears were ringing from the gunshot, and the man beside her managed to sound sincere, even though he was a liar and a murderer.

"I'm done," he continued. "Giving up stealing. When I came here, I merely wanted to find Angela's jewels. Those combined with what I've squirreled away from my other heists mean I can live a life of luxury. I could see spending my retirement with Emily. She came with a lodge—lots of money invested there with good returns. I could do what I wanted, when I wanted, and grow old with someone by my side who adored me."

His grip tightened on Rachel's arm, drawing a faint squeal of pain.

"What made this the right time for retirement?" she asked tightly, every word an effort.

"The dealer I had passed away. I no longer have or need a client to sell my goods to. I'm rich beyond my wildest dreams. Going after Angela's jewelry was a loose end, an expensive mistake. How she figured out I was keeping my identity from her, I'll never know. I killed her before I realized the jewelry wasn't in our safe. Months, years, went by. Then came the article in the newspaper about Shelley David's missing watch. Yes, I kept up with the town—checked the website, read the newspaper, kept hoping something would come up. And then it did."

"You're not going to get away with this," Rachel said.

"I'm giving Cody five more minutes, then I'm leaving, and I'm taking you with me."

Rachel hadn't thought it possible, but Hammonds's grip tightened even more.

"When I think of all the time I spent with Bob, taking him to breakfast and walking around this property listening to his endless, pointless stories." Hammonds groaned. "It wasn't until the wedding shower that I realized it was all right here in the mine shaft."

Rachel longed for her headache to go away, and for his grip to loosen so her circulation would resume and she could try once more to escape.

"When I got here yesterday morning, Bob was nowhere in sight. I waited a while, tore apart both the mobile home and cabin, and finally left. When I got back to the lodge, I began to hear bits and pieces of what was going on. I packed, went out the back, and started following

Chief Becker. I figure it would be him or Cody who'd lead me to Bob, and I was right."

"Lucky you," Rachel croaked. She realized something, and a chill crept up her spine. "You're telling me all this because you're going to kill me. You wouldn't be telling me otherwise."

"Correct," Hammonds said with a sinister grin.

18

"Wrong," Cody growled.

Hammonds whirled at the sound, raising his gun.

Cody took aim. He had one shot, and he didn't intend for even the heat of a bullet to graze Rachel.

Bang!

Hammonds's face contorted, his hand dropped, and there was another loud report.

Rachel shrieked and collapsed to the ground, Hammonds going with her.

Before Cody could get to Rachel, Hammonds struggled to stand.

A black, beige, and brown blur hurtled into him. Timber's jaw clamped down on the hand holding the gun, and Hammonds yowled.

Cody rushed to Rachel's side and lifted her from the snow, cradling her head. Chief Becker was on his knees, cuffing Hammonds. Then Becker moved to Rachel, taking off his coat and turning it into a cushion to elevate her foot.

"Y-you need to keep your coat on," Rachel stuttered.

He gave her a wry smile. "Believe me, I'm not cold."

Timber limped to her side.

"Down," Rachel ordered her dog. "Cody, is he hurt?"

"He doesn't seem to be, but we'll get him to the vet and have him checked out just in case."

Timber settled against Rachel's side. Like Cody, he had no intention of leaving her.

"Am I okay?" Rachel murmured.

"Remember Hammonds threatening to shoot you?" Cody asked.

"Hmmm."

"Well, he did. I shot him in the shoulder, and he shot you in the foot. Then Timber steel-trapped his wrist."

"Good boy," Rachel murmured.

"Hey, why do I always get second billing?" Cody teased.

"How do you know I didn't mean you?" she answered. "Someone should be with Bob."

"We already have him as comfortable as we can make him. He'll be fine. I had some granola bars and a bottle of water on me in case we found him, so he's had those. Besides, he'd never forgive me if I didn't take care of you."

"I'm glad he's okay." Rachel smiled.

"He's pretty impressive at his age with a broken leg, trapped in a mine for almost two days. Believe it or not, Bob found his missing phone down there and even remembered he had a portable charger."

"And Chief Becker, you're okay?"

"You have my winter jacket. I have my Kevlar jacket. Hammonds's bullet didn't have a chance. The fall knocked the wind out of me—that's all."

"We have more police and an ambulance on their way," Cody added, putting his cap on her head.

"Guess I'll never wear heels again," Rachel quipped, gesturing to her wounded foot.

"Right, like you ever wear heels."

"I mean, I'd like the option." She smiled and closed her eyes.

"Where's the ambulance?" Cody asked the chief.

"I'd say two minutes out."

When the ambulance arrived, Rachel went from the snow to a

stretcher. Cody followed, and it only took one look from him to the head paramedic to convince the EMT that yes, the dog was allowed to ride along.

When Rachel opened her eyes, Cody was asleep in a chair next to her hospital bed.

"Hey." She tapped him on the shoulder.

He shot up, groggy, but immediately alert when his eyes focused on her. "How are you feeling?"

"I won't lie. I've been better. You?"

"Same." Rachel realized she wasn't in urgent care, but at the tiny hospital near the edge of town. "Where's my family?"

"Emily insisted that I stay with you. They're in the waiting room."

"How long was I asleep?"

"A few hours. Whatever they gave you while working on your foot was pretty powerful."

Rachel made a face. "Healing from this isn't going to be fun. I don't sit and do nothing very well. Is Bob here too?"

"Yes, he's going to be here for a while between the broken leg, the dehydration, and goodness knows what else. But he's a tough old bird, and he'll be fine. Told me to thank you for saving his life."

"That was more you than me," she protested.

"Actually, I think it was mostly Timber. I don't think we ever would have found him otherwise."

"How is Timber?"

"Most likely sleeping. He has a couple of wounds, but they weren't deep. Timber is strong. Like you."

"Thanks."

"When you're feeling better, you're going to need to make a statement for the police. I hear Hammonds confessed pretty much everything to you."

Remembering, Rachel shivered. "He did it so matter-of-factly. Like he didn't even care about the people he'd hurt along the way."

"He's in custody now. Monica has her family's entire legal team staying at the lodge. I hear they're building quite a case. And it's believed that George Henderson may have accidentally witnessed Hammonds murdering Angela and become collateral damage. It's only a matter of time before he confesses to the murder and gives up the location of George's remains. Then the Hendersons can bury their son, and they and Kristin can finally get the closure they deserve."

"So many people hurt, including you." She traced a raw scratch trailing down the left side of his jaw. "How did you get out of the mine?"

"There was an underground tunnel. Bob couldn't get to it because of his broken leg, but he sent Becker and me through it while you kept Hammonds busy. We would have gotten to you sooner, but we were navigating rocks, an old railcar, ancient scaffoldings, and a sea of scattered tools and litter."

"Sounds like fun. And you got there just in time."

His eyes watered. "I was so scared," he whispered.

Without thinking, she reached out to brush away an errant tear trickling down his cheek. "Of what?" When he didn't answer, she pressed, "You're not scared of anything."

Cody dropped his gaze.

She decided to give him a break. "And Angela's jewels were down there?"

"What Bob hadn't given away. I don't think we'll ever know what motivated her to entrust Bob with her jewels on day two of her honeymoon and not call her family, but that's what she did. Before he went into surgery, Bob told Chief Becker that Angela showed up at his house, handing him a locked box and a letter, and made him promise not to tell anyone. Before Bob could tell Angela that he can't read, she dashed off."

"I didn't know Bob can't read." Rachel closed her eyes for a moment, imagining Bob all alone down in the mine. "Why did he start giving away the jewels?"

"You know Bob. He'd opened that box. But after a year with no sign of Angela—well, in his mind the jewels became his. I'm sure he got confused when Monica asked about them."

"You think Grandma Nettie purchased the Ankar set to help Bob out?"

"Makes as much sense as anything else. We'll know more when we find the letter. And we'll do our best to recover Angela's jewelry and return it to Sheila, to remember her sister by."

"I'm glad we found him."

"Me too," Cody said. Then, his voice grew husky. "It's important to find the people you care about and keep them safe."

She touched his hand. "You rode in the ambulance with me."

"Timber too."

The hospital room was quiet. Rachel had a hard time taking her eyes off Cody. She'd planned to leave the day after the wedding. Now she didn't want to, and it wasn't because of her foot.

"Can I ask you a question?" Maybe now was the perfect time to delve into the past. If it made him uncomfortable, she'd blame whatever medication the doctor had given her.

"Anything."

"Why did Emily break up with you?"

He hesitated, then spoke slowly, carefully. "When I asked her, she laughed and said I was too much like a brother, but the words were rehearsed. I can still remember the look in her eyes." He peered into her face. "She knew that I was in love with you."

Rachel took a breath, feeling like she'd just come alive, like she might never stop smiling. "I think I loved you too."

"And now?"

"I never stopped, Cody. I've always loved you."

He left the chair and came toward the hospital bed, sitting on the edge, careful not to move her foot. "We wasted a lot of time, Rachel. I don't want to waste any more." Taking her in his arms, he leaned in to kiss her lips. "I'm really good at finding jewelry. What would you say if I found you a ring?" He took her left hand in his. "You could wear it here."

She beamed up at him. "I could."

"Hurry up and say yes," came her mother's voice from the doorway. "The whole family's waiting to visit."

"Yes," Rachel said.

From the cheers that erupted in the hallway, Rachel could tell it was more than only her family eavesdropping on her and Cody. It sounded like half the town.

"I like it when I close a case this way," Cody whispered in her ear.

Rachel smiled. She liked it too.